FAIRY TALES, FABLES AND OTHER SHORT STORIES

Collection 1

Fairy Tales, Fables and Other Short Stories

Collection 1

Jordan B. Jolley

Luminare Press
www.luminarepress.com

Fairy Tales, Fables and Other Short Stories

Printed in the United States of America

Cover Design: Melissa K. Thomas

Luminare Press
442 Charnelton St.
Eugene, OR 97401
www.luminarepress.com

ISBN: 978-1-64388-155-3
LCCN: 2019941770

As Always,
Special Thanks to my Family and
their Loving Support

Table of Contents

Introduction *1*

The Peeping Wizard 3

Two Foxes 16

Wezenkap 23

The Bell Tower 31

Wilt & the Witch 39

The Unicorn 45

Thief & Victim 53

Rollins 59

Free Grøls 65

The Long Week 68

Lupendax 75

Michael's Trial 80

Introduction

We often view traditional fairy tales as short, whimsical, folk stories that take place "once upon a time". What usually comes to mind with this introductory phrase is a magical land far far away, often resembling Medieval or Renaissance Europe. Technically, the phrase "once upon a time" means "it happened long ago" or "in the past". Many well-known fairy tales are not set in any specific time period and can be relevant to any era in the past.

Most of us know the classic fairy tales brought to life by the Brothers Grimm, Hans Christian Anderson, and other past storytellers. Their famous tales have been immortalized in our western culture. They are told and re-told, and many times with personal twists and tellings. Folklore tends to do this, and even these stories have roots in earlier works. But as impactful and enjoyable as these tales are, the tales you are about to read in this book are original and bear no direct resemblance to the Grimms' or Anderson's works, though they have had their fair share of influence from past folklore and scriptural references.

There are twelve stories in this book. Some of them, as you will probably notice, mention a world called Elsov, and its inhabitants such as nymphs, dwarves, grøls, etc. The world of Elsov is a reference to the second earth in THE TALES OF DRACO, but the stories here are stand-alone tales and do not require the reading of other books for understanding. However, more information concerning Elsov and its people and creatures can be found in the first book of THE TALES OF DRACO: *Rise of the Dragon*, and its upcoming sequel: *The Six Pieces*.

The tales you are about to read each contain particular morals, themes, and lessons. I hope you will enjoy these stories and that you will cherish their morals.

Jordan B. Jolley

The Peeping Wizard

Once upon a time, on a world called Elsov, there was a colony of nymphs who lived in a land called Pearl Forest. The nymphs of this colony are often a happy folk. Some of them live in houses on the forest floor while many live in the trees. To a newcomer's eyes, their fine wooden houses which hang from the canopy appear as if the nymphs are one with the trees. Vines and leaves cover these houses, making them almost invisible. In the autumn season, when the leaves turn from dark green to bright red or yellow, the houses become a little more noticeable. As many paths as there are on the forest floor, there are just as many wooden bridges connecting the treetop houses and businesses. Some of the sturdy trees have ladders carved into their trunks. Other places, such as under homes, have simple rope ladders.

These nymphs despise anything evil or even related to evil. They are a peaceful and conservative people. They enjoy the forest; never do they wish for another environment. Saying these nymphs are spirits of the woods would not be wrong. But like any other person or creature, they are prone to pride and, dare I say, greed.

Over recent years, hard times had fallen upon the nymphs of Pearl Forest. Since the elven nation suffered a late economic downturn, very few trade carts came to the nymph colony. The nymphs had very little to trade and even less to expect in return. They needed to rely on themselves for survival. They ate their own crops, made their own tools, and traded amongst themselves. Their currency was next to worthless. Most shops and businesses were closed. But, and this may come as no surprise, few nymphs left the colony.

It was a hard time, no question about that, but it was far from a sad time. The nymphs relied on nature for happiness, and no economy was going to affect their enchanted forest. Magic was, and still is, a part of Pearl Forest. Even though the nymphs were poor, they were blessed with good food and good homes.

So, you see that most nymphs were happy with their lives then. But not all of them ignored wealth. There was one such nymph who wished to be wealthy. Autumn Leaf was his name. He was not a greedy nor a deceptive nymph. All he wanted was fortune, nothing more. (Have we not all had this same desire at some point in our lives?) Autumn Leaf's mother told him to enjoy life as it was, but Autumn Leaf could not enjoy the magic and beauty that Pearl Forest had to offer without thinking about money in his pockets. There was nothing he wanted to purchase; he only wanted great wealth.

"Why do you not enjoy what you have?" Autumn Leaf's mother once asked him.

"I do not want to appear greedy, Mother, I really do not," said Autumn Leaf. "All I wish is to not be poor."

"Well, our time shows no mercy on us, my Son," his mother replied. "It is not a force that is in our hands. The elves have faced hostility that their economy cannot handle. Besides, wealth can change you like a wraith's bite if you are not careful. Wealth is a stepping stone to pride. It can easily corrupt you."

"I plan to share my wealth, Mother."

"And that is a good thought. But as I have said, this is not a force that is in our hands. How about you take a walk down the path? The forest air can refresh your mind."

Autumn Leaf sighed. "Very well."

His mother kissed him on the cheek. Autumn Leaf opened the front door and crossed the porch to a rope ladder.

"Remember to be home by twilight, and take care of yourself," his mother said as he descended.

"I will!" he called back.

Autumn Leaf stretched his little arms before making his way down the main path. Before long, not a single house was seen, not even in the trees. Autumn Leaf was alone. He took a deep breath. The cool air felt refreshing in his lungs. A while later, Autumn Leaf stopped by the pond that was near the point where his path merged with a much longer one. The pond's water sparkled glittering blue.

Autumn Leaf felt at ease. As he splashed some of the cold water on his face, he heard singing off in the woods. The words sounded foreign. Autumn Leaf stood to find a figure approaching him. It hovered over the pond, its wings flowing like a soft melody. It appeared to be a woman with a long blue dress, soft brown hair, and long gentle wings. It was a curious fairy. And what a beautiful fairy she was! The songs of other fairies could be heard close by. This one fairy seemed too shy to talk to the nymph. Neither of them spoke. The fairy gave a fragile smile, then she cast a few green and blue orbs that circled over Autumn Leaf's head. When Autumn Leaf tried to touch one of the orbs, it flew back to the fairy like a frightened offspring returning to its mother. Autumn Leaf eventually smiled as well. All his concerns in life seemed to be masked at that moment. Even his want for wealth was momentarily pacified, which took a lot of power to do.

It was some time before the fairy fluttered away. Autumn Leaf did not know for sure how long the fairy was there. The sun was still up, so Autumn Leaf decided to continue on his walk. The songs from the other fairies slowly faded to silence. Now all Autumn Leaf could hear was the humming of insects and the singing of birds. The pond was calm, and some of the orbs were still floating under the sparkling blue water.

Autumn Leaf began to believe that he did not need wealth to be happy. His life was good enough. After meeting the shy fairy, what more could he ask for? No money could buy such a pleasant experience.

The nymph continued happily down the road until it reached the merge. He could either go left or right. He took a quick look down the left side. That way led to the swamplands. Autumn Leaf did not dare go there. The swamp was home to many dangers. He could stumble across some grumpy and barbaric ogre, or he could get stuck or even sink in swamp goo! The many mosquitoes may suck his blood dry. The path may even disappear into a thick bog, making it easy to get lost. Autumn Leaf remembered that an experienced guide from his colony and a mysterious dark-scaled dragon had once disappeared in there. Most believed they were captured. Not many believed the dragon harmed the nymph since the dragon was friendly. Autumn Leaf did not even consider taking the left path. He took the right.

The dark thoughts of the swamplands soon faded from his mind. He again had the same feelings as when he had met the fairy. Life could not get any better. It was late noon when Autumn Leaf considered turning around, but first he wanted to round a bend before heading home. As he approached the bend, a strange sensation washed over him. He no longer heard the insects or birds. He could hear nothing save the breeze in the trees. It was a lonely feeling.

How funny, thought Autumn Leaf. It feels like I am headed to the swamplands, except I am not.

Autumn Leaf felt the strong urge to immediately turn around, so he did. He had barely taken five steps in the other direction when he heard a voice say, "Good afternoon, my little nymph."

Autumn Leaf nearly jumped out of his skin. He looked to where the voice had come from. There was a tall, thin man who sat on a boulder off to the side of the path. The man was dressed in various shades of green and gray. Though he wore no cloak, Autumn Leaf believed he was a wizard of some sort. No one else could surprise a nymph in such a manner.

"Eh… a good noon to you too, sir," Autumn Leaf stuttered.

The man chuckled. "Ah! Pardon me for such an unnecessary scare, but I know your troubles. Times aren't easy nowadays. Many are poor, few are rich."

"I have sought wealth, sir, I must admit. But I believe I do not need such money anymore," said Autumn Leaf.

"I see. I see," said the man, slowly rubbing his hands. "Have you ever wondered what being rich is like?"

"I have."

"Then you must understand the power you may have?"

"What power?" asked Autumn Leaf.

"Why, the power over your brethren, of course! You would be the only wealthy nymph in your colony."

Autumn Leaf thought for a moment. "I can envision what you are saying… to a level, least to say."

"Good," said the man. "As you may have noticed, I am a wizard. I know of a place that's filled with treasure. It will grant you the wealth you dream of and maybe beyond that. As a wizard, if you follow me, your wishes will be granted."

"Would this treasure not be more helpful to people like the dwarves? They may need it more than I do," said Autumn Leaf. "Nymphs need no riches. We rely on the forest."

The wizard stepped down from the boulder. He was a good foot-and-a-half taller than the nymph. "When you have the treasure, you may do whatever with it. Keep it or give it away. Besides, I thought you sought wealth for yourself."

"Well, I did. But then I…" Autumn Leaf stared at the wizard. The man seemed serious. After a brief moment of silence, Autumn Leaf said, "What is there to lose?"

The wizard smiled. "Now you understand, my little nymph. Come with me and I'll show you the way to the great treasure. My powers as a wizard are great."

The strange wizard started up the path as if he was headed to Autumn Leaf's colony. Autumn Leaf followed him. When they reached the point where the path branched off to the colony, the wizard kept going straight. Autumn Leaf stopped. "You do not intend to go into the swamplands, do you?"

"Yes," said the wizard, not turning around to give his answer.

Autumn Leaf gulped. "Is it safe to go there?"

"I'm a man of magic. We'll be safe."

"You do not even have a Master Scepter: a wizard's greatest tool."

Reaching into one of his pockets, the wizard held out a carved wand for Autumn Leaf to see. It was a magic albore.

"This is all we will need. No need to worry."

Autumn Leaf sighed. He looked down the path to the swamplands, then down the path to his home.

"Well?" said the wizard.

Autumn Leaf set his eyes back on the path to the swamplands. "I am coming." He followed the wizard down the east-bound way when something crossed his mind. "What is your name, wizard?"

"Does my name matter?" asked the wizard. "Is it treasure you seek or useless knowledge?"

"Forget I asked," said Autumn Leaf. He tried not to show that he was offended.

He followed the wizard down the path in silence. Soon enough, the air became humid. Sweat began running down Autumn Leaf's forehead. The humming of insects came to his ears again, except this time it was louder than before; and far more annoying. And they were not bees that Autumn Leaf heard, but rather a mix of many insects: mosquitoes, cicadas, and other species he did not recognize. The mosquitoes buzzed around the nymph's head like tiny devils. Autumn Leaf tried smacking them, but that did no good. The wizard pulled something from one of the pockets in his tunic. It was a vial that held some white cream.

"Rub this on your skin. It will keep the mosquitoes away," the wizard directed.

The cream kept the insects away, fortunately, but Autumn Leaf did not feel any better. Not long after, he began hearing other noises. A low howl echoed through the moist air. Autumn Leaf nervously stayed close behind the wizard, not uttering a word. The path soon led them to an open bog. The setting sun's reflection in the dewdrops nearly blinded Autumn Leaf. The wizard continued into the bog, as if he was unaware of how soggy the ground was. Though a walk through the bog was not a pleasant experience for a wizard, it could still be done. For a nymph, however, it was next to impossible. Autumn Leaf could hardly take one step after another. He was not even halfway across the bog when the wizard reached the other side. Then came something Autumn Leaf feared he would meet. As he struggled, two monsters emerged from the shadows at the bog's edge. Both were large and had green skin. Their bellies were round and their smell was unbearable. He had never seen monsters like them before, but Autumn Leaf knew for sure that they were ogres. What else would they be? Before Autumn Leaf could take another step, the two ogres raced after him. They moved across the bog as if they were trampling over a field of daisies. They made hideous gurgling noises as they ran. Autumn Leaf realized that there was nothing he could do, so he waved his arms in panic. "Help me, wizard! Help me!"

The wizard quickly pulled out his albore. In less than a second, a small violet explosion erupted in the ogres' path. Both fell face-first into the swampy ground. Autumn Leaf grimaced from the sloppy waves that ran up his body following the splash. When the ogres returned to their feet, the wizard cast a lightning bolt at the monsters. They immediately ran after the wizard instead, making the deep howl that Autumn Leaf had heard before. Their steps splashed more thick goo onto Autumn Leaf. Another lightning bolt told the ogres to run or face something worse. They both lumbered off, gurgling in disappointment. Shaken by the encounter with the ogres, Autumn Leaf swam to dry ground where the wizard was waiting. The nymph was disgusted by the slime that covered his body. Now he smelled as foul as the ogres! Luckily, the wizard cast another spell. A warm sensation ran up Autumn Leaf's legs and the slime evaporated. Soon, other than his racing heart, Autumn Leaf felt as if the ogres had never attacked him at all.

"Thank you," he said. "You saved my life."

The wizard did not say anything. He simply nodded before continuing down the path. This time Autumn Leaf walked beside him rather than behind.

“I thought I was in the stew when those two nasty ogres attacked,” said Autumn Leaf.

“You will be filled with much more gratitude at the end of our journey, my little nymph,” the wizard replied.

Autumn Leaf was grateful for sure. Every minute that passed offered him more trust in the unknown wizard. He had little concern … until dusk arrived. Autumn Leaf remembered the promise he had given to his mother. He was nowhere near his home. He and the wizard had crossed a great distance on foot, and through the swamplands no-less! By now they were out of the worst of it. When they reached the great river, the wizard’s path made a perpendicular turn to the northwest. By the time they were out of the swamplands completely, it was well into the night. The wizard soon stopped to let Autumn Leaf rest. But Autumn Leaf did not rest. He was worried about his mother.

“Wizard, I promised my mother that I would return home by twilight.”

“Is that the cause of all your worry?” asked the wizard, almost sounding as if he was mocking Autumn Leaf.

“I believe she is worried about me.”

The wizard fiddled with the albore in his pocket. “If you bring your wealth home the following day, your mother will understand. Either you return with your wealth and she is pleased, or you return as poor as you are now and she is upset since you are late. You cannot turn back now and be on time. No matter when you return home, her worries will go.”

Autumn Leaf thought about the wizard’s words. He did have a point. His mother’s worries would leave no matter how late he was. He might as well make her happy rather than upset. He gave a quick yawn and said, “Let us continue.”

The wizard did so with Autumn Leaf beside him. They were out of the swamp, but the nymph began to hear howling again. This time it came from wolves, not ogres. Autumn Leaf grew tense. “How much further?” he asked.

The wizard stopped and pointed forward. Up ahead was a single hill. At its base was a three-level house. The house looked very old. It had a wooden frame, and the shingles on the roof were ruined. Some of the short pillars in the line that wrapped around the porch were missing. From what celestial light Autumn Leaf had, he noticed that many of the windows had cracked or shattered panes. The house had to have been abandoned if it was in such a sorry condition. Autumn Leaf did not like it one bit.

"Your treasure is in the basement," the wizard informed. "I'll stay here. You go on inside."

"Why must you stay out here?" Autumn Leaf questioned.

The wizard did not answer. He simply motioned Autumn Leaf to go inside the house.

Autumn Leaf gulped and headed to the house alone. I hope this treasure is worth coming here, he thought. He told himself that there was no need to be scared. There should not be any danger or else the wizard would have followed him in.

There was no front door in the frame, so Autumn Leaf just walked in the house. There was no noise save the sound of scurrying mice, maybe rats. There was no furniture anywhere, which proved to Autumn Leaf that the house was abandoned. As he looked for the entrance to the basement, he realized that he was not excited all. His wish for wealth was about to come true! Why was he not excited? Then Autumn Leaf thought about the wizard. The nymph did not recognize him. He had heard of other wizards who were very friendly. This wizard was more of a peeping wizard: one whom a foolish person would seek for foolish desires. These peeping wizards were often mysterious, selfish, and sly people. Autumn Leaf started questioning his trust and choice to follow the wizard when he finally found stairs to the basement. They were behind a rotting door.

Now it was time to see if he would really be wealthy … or if he was walking into a trap.

When Autumn Leaf descended the stairs, he saw rows after rows of wooden chests next to the wall. In the center of the walkway was a burning torch that gave him just enough light to see. There was an intersecting walkway just beyond the torch. Why the torch was burning in an abandoned house, Autumn Leaf did not know. He decided not to worry about that. He opened one of the chests instead.

The moment of truth.

A tear formed in his eye. He saw the glimmer of rubies, diamonds, emeralds, and saphires! Autumn Leaf opened another chest that was filled with gold and silver coins. Autumn Leaf slammed the lid shut in excitement. All these chests were filled with treasure! What a night! The sorrows from his experience with the ogres vanished into thin air.

"I am a wealthy nymph! I am a wealthy nymph!" he cried.

He was on his way back up the stairs. He wanted to thank the wizard for granting his wish. Maybe trusting in a strange wizard was not as bad as he thought. But halfway up the steps, he heard a noise behind him. It sounded like huffing. Then came the sound of rustling chains. Autumn Leaf returned to the basement. The sound came from the other walkway where he could not see. The huffing was getting louder. Autumn Leaf turned the corner and stopped dead in his tracks. The hair on his arms stood straight. The next tear in his eye was out of fear, not joy. In front of him was a yawning beast. It appeared to be waking up. A metal ring was strapped around its neck, and several chains were hung on the ring. The beast was much bigger than Autumn Leaf. It had gray scales, white horns, sharp teeth, and broad wings. It was a large darkscaled dragon, chained in the treasure room as if it were the dragon's dungeon! Autumn Leaf shivered at such a terrible sight.

When the dragon blinked a few times, it set its amber eyes on Autumn Leaf and began growling. It then gave a menacing roar that filled the room. Autumn Leaf covered his ears. After the roar, he saw the dragon's yellow eyes glowing. It opened its jaws to expose the fire forming in its throat. Autumn Leaf had just enough time to jump behind the corner of the other walkway when the wave of fire blew past him. The basement's chill was suddenly replaced by intense heat. Autumn Leaf's face felt as if it was burning. The dragon cast the terrible flame for a full minute before it stopped. The torch was burnt to ashes, but several of the chests were on fire, making the room much brighter. Hot coins and jewels spilled onto the floor.

Autumn Leaf could not escape through the house, lest he should walk back in the dragon's path of fire. If he gave the dragon even the slightest chance, it would eat him in two bites. A nymph alone was no match for such a terrible monster. Autumn Leaf looked down the other end of the walkway. To his relief, he saw another set of stairs going up. He covered his ears when the dragon roared again. As another wave of furious flames blew past him, he made his way to the stairs. The dragon's roar was too loud, even there. He climbed the stairs where he reached a closed trapdoor that was held by a short, metal beam. Autumn Leaf pulled it out, pushed the trapdoor open, and climbed to the surface. With his cheeks covered in tears and sweat, he found himself on the side of the hill some distance from the house. Autumn Leaf ran to where the wizard was waiting. The wizard almost appeared surprised when he saw Autumn Leaf running towards him from the hill.

"There is a dragon chained up in the treasure room!" Autumn Leaf cried.

The wizard remained silent for a moment. "So, you have seen the dragon and lived. It was supposed to kill you."

Autumn Leaf could not believe his ears. "It *was* a trap!"

"Indeed, it was."

Another tear ran down Autumn Leaf's face. "If you wanted me dead, why did you not let the ogres kill me? Why lead me here?"

"It was all a part of my plan," the wizard answered with a simple shrug.

"But… why?"

"My nature." The wizard pulled out his albore. "I kept that savage dragon hungry. I wanted you to be his next meal. I must admit, I didn't believe you would come out alive. Now I must feed the dragon myself."

Autumn Leaf tried to run, but a surge of energy shocked him. Before he knew it, he was on the ground. The wizard created another spell from the albore that started dragging Autumn Leaf closer to the old house. Autumn Leaf panicked. No matter how hard he tried to escape, the invisible force had complete control over him. He slid over the rough dirt. There was nothing he could do. All he thought about was how foolish he was for trusting an unknown wizard, all for the sake of wealth. How foolish! But before he reached the porch, he heard the sound of breaking floorboards. A glow appeared inside the house, then the front was suddenly destroyed. Pieces of wood and glass landed all around Autumn Leaf. The dragon had charged through the doorway with its horns. It was loose! There was nothing keeping it chained anymore! The dragon stared at Autumn Leaf. The nymph stared back. Its eyes were not glowing, which meant it was not going to breathe fire. Autumn Leaf still expected a terrible end by tooth and claw, but the dragon did not attack him. It spread its large brown wings and took flight. The brief gust of wind raced past the helpless nymph. Autumn Leaf looked ahead. It was not after him, it was after the wizard! He saw the frightened man turn and run into the forest just before the dragon sent down a fiery storm. The wizard was out of sight when the dragon landed and ran on foot.

A bright orange light flickered behind a grove of trees, then Autumn Leaf was free.

He quickly stood up and ran into the opposite grove. He barely reached the trees when he saw the gray dragon back in the sky. It held something in its mouth. Autumn Leaf presumed it was part of the wizard's shirt. The dragon dropped the torn garment and cast fire over the house that was already burning from the inside. The entire house was engulfed in seconds. The dragon circled over the house until it collapsed, then the beast flew off into the night. All that was left were burning piles of wood and a pillar of smoke that could be seen for miles. Autumn Leaf did not stay. He did not care about whatever treasure was left behind in the fire. He left immediately, but did not know where the path home was. He ran into the forest until he was out of breath, then he sat next to a tree trunk and wept. He wept for a long time. He no longer wanted wealth, he wanted to go home. As he continued weeping, he heard something nearby. It sounded like someone was humming a sweet tune. When Autumn Leaf looked up, he saw the blue fairy approaching him from the thick of the forest. It was the same fairy he had met before meeting the wizard. The fairy seemed to be weeping too, her tears were like glittering crystals.

"I have made such a terrible decision," said Autumn Leaf. "I should not have trusted a peeping wizard. I did not know who he was and I followed him anyway for such a silly reason."

The fairy continued humming her soft tune. It was the same tune the other fairies hummed at the pond. Autumn Leaf remembered his feelings then. He remembered that he was a nymph. Nymphs relied on the forest, not wealth. Most of the nymphs were poor, but the magic of Pearl Forest was enough to make them happy.

"Fairy, can you guide me home?" Autumn Leaf pleaded.

The fairy nodded. She fluttered through the woods with Autumn Leaf walking below. They took no paths, for Autumn Leaf was going straight home. He was not any richer than he was before. He was only happy, even if he had to explain himself to his mother.

Does this story have a happy ending? That is up to you to decide.

Two Foxes

The young rabbit lived quite a peaceful life. She had many brothers and sisters and extended family in her warren. But to her, it was never overwhelming. The rabbit was either in her burrow, eating, or enjoying the meadow where she lived. She never dared wander too far from her home, though. There was no telling what sort of dangers would be out there waiting for her. There were stoats, weasels, humans, and, of course, foxes. The rabbit had learned all about these dangers from her elders ever since she first left her burrow.

Although she was warned every time she went outside, the gray-furred rabbit never imagined she would confront any of these predators. That all changed soon enough. One day, as she was feeding in the meadow, a strange sound reached her keen rabbit ears.

Something was nearby.

Instinct told her she should flee immediately. She was about to leave, but it was too late. She was suddenly face to face with a red fox! Oh, how cruel fate can be for luring it here! The rabbit prepared to run when the fox took a step back.

"Don't be afraid, rabbit. I mean you no harm," said the fox, clearly a vixen.

The rabbit did not believe the fox. "Why would you not want to harm me? I'm a rabbit."

"I understand," said the fox. "But you must understand this: there is instinct, and there is choice, and I choose not to attack. I want to warn you; other foxes will come by. Remain underground, as you often do. Just remember to stay as far apart as you can.

Never crowd everyone together, and keep as far from the surface as possible."

The rabbit stared into the vixen's auburn eyes. She could not tell if the fox was a creature to trust or not. Foxes were predators after all. But what if this particular one was not lying? What if there were other foxes out there?

"How do I know you are telling the truth?" the rabbit asked.

"I cannot prove what I know," said the fox. "It is up to you to believe me."

With her message given, the fox bounded off into the brush and was gone in a second. The rabbit was left to ponder. She did not know how to tell if the fox was telling the truth or not. Confused and terrified, she decided to go home. That night she told her father about the encounter with the unusual vixen.

"Quite funny for a fox to say that," her father said.

"Yes, but I don't know if she was telling the truth," replied the rabbit.

Her father's ears twitched, a sign that he was thinking. After a moment of silence he said, "Hmm... Maybe for the next few days, we should be more careful than usual. That's all we can do, I guess."

The next day went by without the scent of a fox, much to the rabbit's relief. Then the day after arrived. That morning, during the rabbit's early meal, the faint sound of sneaking vulpes came again. At first the rabbit believed it was the vixen from before. But after a few sniffs, she knew otherwise. The rabbit turned for home when she finally caught sight of another fox! This second one was also a vixen. Her orange fur was gritty, especially on the right side of her face, which had an old scab. She looked as if she had been through a nasty fight. Crouching low, her eyes straight on her target, she looked like she was ready to pounce. The rabbit took off in the other direction, ready to spread the alarm. She was not too far off when she heard the fox shouting at her to stop and that she wanted to talk to her. The rabbit stopped and turned around. The fox caught up to her.

"Your whole family is in danger," said the fox. "You must stay together as one. Make sure you are near the surface so you can hear the danger coming."

The rabbit was about to leave to tell her father when she remembered what had happened the day before yesterday. The first fox had told her to keep her family as spread out as possible, and to stay away from the surface. This second one was telling her to do something completely different.

"What danger will be coming?" the rabbit decided to ask.

"Why, other foxes of course," the vixen answered. "They may come very soon, so hurry!"

"But another fox told me to have my warren stay underground and far apart from one another," said the rabbit.

"When?"

"The day before yesterday."

The fox snarled in an unpleasant manner. The rabbit was ready to run. She could not stand to see such terrible teeth that could end her life in a single snap.

"That other fox was the one you should beware! She was lying to you. Keeping your family far apart would mean more to pick off. Lives will be lost!"

The rabbit considered the new information. "I understand what you're saying," she said.

"Good. Remember to get your family close together. That other deceitful menace will come. You must tell your family now! Hurry! Hurry!"

The rabbit ran for the burrow. It almost seemed like the fox was ready to pursue her, but she turned and bounded off instead. When the rabbit reached her home, she decided not to tell anyone just yet. A thought entered her mind, a thought that sickened her mind. The second fox said the first one was lying. But what if she was lying herself? The rabbit did not know what to do. She did not know who was right. Trusting the wrong fox could mean the end of her home and family!

She remained silent for the rest of the evening; there was no need to scare the children. The next day she returned to the meadow with caution. Any sudden noise would cause her to jump. Any new scent would make her want to flee. Clouds filled the sky and a light rain began to fall. Then the fox came. It was the first fox. This made the rabbit feel uneasy. What if the second fox was telling the truth? She could be staring at death itself!

"Have you told your warren what do?" asked the fox.

"Not yet…" The rabbit had a hard time explaining. "I met… another fox yesterday. She told me to bring my family close together and to stay near the surface."

The fox was silent for a moment. Not once did she snarl or yip out of anxiety. She seemed concerned. "I told you to watch out for many dangers. That vixen you met yesterday is the most dangerous of them all."

"Are you saying that *she's* the liar?"

"Yes. She has the tongue of a snake. Beware if she comes back. Your best chance for your family is if you do what I say. Don't go anywhere near the surface until she is gone. Stay apart from one another underground." The fox then stared off to the left, her eyes wide and ears standing. "Remember what I said. Please do."

Then the fox was off. The rabbit was left alone. Her poor mind was running like… a rabbit!

"I don't know who to believe!" she wailed. "There's danger about and it is in disguise! One of those foxes is lying. They can't both be telling the truth."

The rabbit knew she should not remain in the open or else she would be asking for a predator's arrival. She returned to her warren where her family was feeding and playing. Her brothers and sisters dashed around her, chasing one another joyfully. Her parents were happily watching their young ones.

"Father, mother, I fear something awful is going to happen," said the rabbit.

"I see you're concerned," said her father. "Is it because of that fox? Is it after us?" He was ready to stamp his foot to alert everyone.

"I met another fox. She said the first is trying to kill us. The first says the same with the second. I don't know who to believe!"

"What did the first fox tell you to do?" her mother asked.

"She said to make sure the rabbits are spread out and to avoid the surface."

"And what about the second?"

"She said that we must stay together and stay near the surface so that we may be alert."

Her mother's right ear twitched like her father's had the other day. "Which do you think is a better idea?"

The rabbit thought. "Well, if the aggressive fox sees us all together and near the surface, she can drag away whichever rabbit she wants, even if we fight back. If we are spread out, she'll have a difficult time trying to dig us up. We can move around easily in the burrows, too."

"Now, how did the first fox behave?" asked her mother.

"The first one seemed quite calm, almost friendly."

"And the second?"

"She seemed forceful. I would say she would not allow us to do anything our way."

"Now think about each one," said her father. "This may sound silly, but I am serious. If each fox was a carrot, which one would be good and which one would be rotten?"

Carrots, thought the rabbit. Which one should she trust? She pondered for some time, but finally had an idea who to trust.

"The first fox is the truthful one," she said with confidence.

"You will know the truth by its fruit," her mother stated.

The rabbit now felt who she should believe. After thanking her parents, the sudden stamp of a foot reached her ears. Rabbits rushed for safety. The rabbit's siblings were now running in fright instead of fun.

"What will we do when the predator comes?" one of the little ones cried.

The rabbit told her kin what to do. Most heeded her and were deep in their burrows. But a few did not listen and joined together near the surface. The rabbit stayed near the burrow to see which fox would come. It was the second fox that had arrived, just as the rabbit predicted. The fox trotted up to the rabbit as if they were close friends. The rabbit wanted to run into her burrow now that she knew she was staring at the deceiver, but she did not want to make the fox suspicious.

"Have you told your warren what to do?" the fox asked.

"I have," said the rabbit.

The fox quickly ran to one of the holes and buried her nose inside it. She then lifted her snout back out and stared angrily at the rabbit. "I see nothing down there!"

The rabbit grew tense. She could not reply. She knew the fox realized her distrust. With a snarl, the fox raced after her. The rabbit, with all her luck, made it far enough into the hole before the vixen's jaws could snatch her out. She was soon met by black paws digging their way towards her. The rabbit burrowed far enough in that the digging was in vain. The fox left her to go to another hole. The rabbit's breathing did not slow until she knew for sure the fox was gone. She stayed where she was, not moving an inch. She sat quietly when she suddenly heard the cries of two foxes. The rabbit did not recognize the noises immediately, so she remained in the burrow, even after the terrible noises had ceased. Then a voice came from the hole.

"She is gone. That aggressive vixen is gone." It was the voice of the first fox.

The rabbit slowly made her way to the surface. The fox was sitting down, licking one of her paws. She was bleeding from her ears and feet, but she was alive. "The other vixen left with two of your rabbits, but the rest have not been harmed," she said. "I had to fight the vixen. She is gone and will never return."

"You… saved our warren!" exclaimed the rabbit. "How can we ever thank you?"

"No thanks is needed," said the fox.

"You can be our guardian," the rabbit suggested. "You've saved our warren and I believe the other rabbits will want you to protect us."

"I would be willing to be your guardian," the fox began. "But alas, I'm a fox. You are a rabbit. I may soon have a family and I must be my children's guardian. It is my nature to eat you. I saved your warren. Now you may prosper."

The rabbit did not reply as the fox ran off. She left the meadow, never to return. The rabbit was sad that two in her warren had died. But the rest had lived, and that made her happy. The rabbit never understood why the fox wanted to save the warren from her own kind. She never saw that fox again, but the rabbit never forgot.

Wezenkap

Nicholas was the bravest and, as many consider, the most selfless dwarf in all the land. He was no official warrior since he lived before the great wars, but Nicholas had done many deeds not many would dare do. Despite his many friends and social life, Nicholas lived alone. Sometimes he would disappear for a few weeks so he could spend some time by himself.

It was on one of these holidays that forever changed Nicholas's life, one that tested his very selfless nature. He sat on the bank of a river while eating a small lunch. The riverbank was his favorite place to go on private holidays. The river ran through the free, rolling hills. There was a constant breeze that formed waves in the green summer grass. Nicholas loved this place very much. He enjoyed the isolation, but he was not too far from civilization. Nicholas knew that down the riverside, about a mile away, there was a grove; and in that grove was a town of grøls: little, jolly folk who lived inside trees as if they were houses.[1] Nicholas had never visited the grøls before. He preferred to leave them be. But on this particular day, after Nicholas had finished his lunch, he noticed something. There was a foul smell in the air. It came from the grøl village, which was unusual. Something was wrong. Never before had Nicholas noticed such an odor. He had to find out what was going on. With only a hand-axe for defense (hence the need may come), he approached the grøl's village from the river bank. He reached the village soon enough. Not a single grøl was present. The doors and windows in

1 More information on grøls is provided in the appendix for *The Tales of Draco: Rise of the Dragon*.

the trees were shut and covered. The smell was even stronger here. It was disgusting! It made Nicholas wince. Nothing extraordinary was present, however. Nicholas approached one of the doors and knocked on it. There was no answer. He was about to knock again when he heard footsteps behind him…

…followed by an eerie cackle.

Nicholas turned to find, in his horror, five sneering goblins! Such hideous and menacing monsters goblins are! They grinned at Nicholas with terrible yellow teeth. The goblin in the center of the group wore a horned helmet of dwarfish make.

Nicholas raised his hand-axe as a gesture of courage. The goblins cackled again.

"Such a deadly weapon," said the sarcastic goblin on the far right.

"It is all I have and it's all I need," Nicholas replied.

The goblins laughed and raised their own weapons. Two had spears, two had spiked maces, and the one with the horned helmet had an old, grimy sword.

"Now to end this poor dwarf's life!" the middle goblin sneered.

They all charged at Nicholas.

Now as I have mentioned earlier, Nicholas was considered to be the bravest in all the land. A wave of fear did wash over our hero, as it would wash over any of us in a similar situation, but it was this very fear that drove Nicholas's courage. He raised his hand-axe high above his head and charged as well. The spear, intended for his heart, struck the door instead. Nicholas returned the advance by slicing the spear shaft with his hand-axe. The other goblins advanced with fierce aggression. Nicholas defended himself the best he could, but he was unable to protect himself from every blow. He was wounded most especially by the maces. Even though he was outnumbered, he fought back as if he was fully healthy. Before he knew it, three goblins lay dead. Only the goblin with the helmet and one with a mace were left. As weary as Nicholas was, he continued to fight. The spiked mace struck his foot when he advanced again. The pain was unbearable, but Nicholas remained standing. He continued to fight until the only enemy standing was the mace-holder. That goblin stopped fighting when he realized he was the only one left. The one with the helmet had fallen.

"Our captain is dead," he growled. "You will pay!"

Nicholas did not reply. The goblin, to his surprise, retreated.

Nicholas could no longer fight back anyway. He did not realize how badly wounded he was until he suddenly collapsed. Mace, spear, and sword wounds riddled his limbs and side. He even felt broken ribs! The pain was soon too much for even the brave dwarf to handle. He passed out. He would have died too, but not long after he fell asleep, the door that suffered the spear opened. Two frightened grøls stepped out, a man and his wife. They were horrified when they saw the carnage. They inspected each body for clues as to what had happened.

"Oh dear, this one's still alive!" said the wife with a shiver after inspecting Nicholas.

The husband rushed over. Nicholas was still breathing. "He must be a dwarf," the husband said. "He fought all these evil beings by himself, no help to speak of!"

The wife picked up the hand-axe. "Such a warrior, I say. He mustn't die. He mustn't!"

"His wounds are deep," said the husband. "We cannot help him."

"The fairies!" exclaimed the wife. "The fairies can heal him. Quick, we must hurry!"

Other grøls emerged from their homes, many still on the lookout for danger. The first two grøls told the rest to quickly fetch a cart. The horse-drawn cart arrived in no time. With great effort, they all had to do their part to place Nicholas inside it. The husband and wife drove the horse away from their village. They left the hand-axe, but the horned helmet lay at the foot of the cart.

Hours later, Nicholas slowly regained consciousness. His head throbbed, but the rest of the pain was gone. He looked down. What were once deep wounds were now mere scars. Nicholas looked up to find a fairy by his side. Her wings did not flow since she stood on the ground. She held a bottle of some sort of healing potion. At first Nicholas thought she was an angel.

"You were at the veil of death," said the fairy.

"You saved my life," said Nicholas wearily. "I will forever be in your debt."

The fairy offered a pleasing smile. "It is we who are in your debt. You have protected the grøls from five goblins with no help. These goblins held high ranks. They would have destroyed the grøls and driven the rest of us out."

Nicholas took a deep breath. "I did what had to be done."

"And we thank you for it." The fairy set the bottle down and presented the helmet to Nicholas. The horns had been removed, leaving two empty sockets. The metal had been polished and was now sparkling. The helmet was dazzling! It looked completely different from before.

"This helmet is enchanted," said the fairy. "Because of your bravery, it will grant you great strength when you wear it. We call it Wezenkap. Please accept it." She placed it on the bed beside Nicholas.

"Wezenkap," said Nicholas, eyeing its glimmering surface. "It is beautiful. But I ask for no reward."

"You do not have to. Please accept it as a gift. It is a token of our thanks."

Nicholas sat up in the bed. He picked up Wezenkap. It certainly was beautiful.

"Thank you," he said. "I'll accept it as your token. I will only use its strength for good."

"It is your strength from which the helmet draws its power," the fairy replied.

Nicholas remained in the bed for another hour until he felt well-rested. The fairy gave him one last farewell and he was on his way home. As he walked, he cradled Wezenkap in his arms as if it was a newborn babe. He was met with great praise in the grøl village when he passed through. All the grøls cheered, shouting many yips of joy. Nicholas was pleased, but he did not stay in the village for long. The grøls understood and let him be after they expressed their gratitude. Nicholas then passed his favorite spot beside the river. About halfway home, he came across several oaks. This gave Nicholas the opportunity to test Wezenkap's power. He placed the helmet on his head. Almost immediately he felt the power pulse through his limbs. He was full of energy! With a grunt, he grabbed hold of an oak trunk. To his pure astonishment, he ripped the whole tree from the ground. It was true! Wezenkap had actually given him great strength! How Nicholas was grateful! The moment he dropped the oak, he truly vowed to only use Wezenkap for good. He returned home with delight.

Weeks passed and Nicholas never used Wezenkap for his own pleasure. He only used it for the benefit of his people. He once rescued a brother and sister from a devastating fire, and later freed a family that was trapped under a rockslide. His greatest deed was when more goblins invaded the grøl village after hearing about the death of their captain. Fifty goblins arrived. Nicholas heard of their coming and returned to the village. Not one of those fifty were successful. Nicholas did not use a single weapon. Wezenkap gave him a great advantage indeed. And all throughout his good deeds, the helmet was always glimmering. Its beauty was always present, even in dim light.

Word of Nicholas and Wezenkap spread, as good stories often do. Soon enough, the story reached the ears of the second goblin captain, ruler of a nasty palisade fort on the rolling hills. This captain knew all he needed to know about Nicholas, for he was the one who had suffered the defeat of fifty goblins. He knew that if Nicholas did not have Wezenkap on his head, he could be defeated if attacked properly. Nicholas could stop five goblins by himself. But if he was trapped in the fort without Wezenkap, he would not stand a chance! The captain thought that that was the only way to stop Nicholas. The problem was getting him to the fort without Wezenkap on his head. That was not a problem to ponder for long. The cunning captain summoned one of his spies. A dwarf. The goblin captain explained his plan and gave the spy not a weapon but a sleeping potion. The spy also altered his appearance so he looked like an honest farmer. His disguise could fool anyone, even though he had no honesty to speak of, and his ideas of farming were only good for the worms. The spy set off for the town where Nicholas lived. Nobody in the town suspected him of any evil intentions. He rode into town on a mule-driven cart, carrying a long wooden box.

Nicholas always kept Wezenkap nearby in case someone needed his help. The strength needed often came when he least expected it. He was in his house when the knock on the door came. Nicholas believed his help was needed again, so he picked up Wezenkap. The helmet glistened in the sunlight that came through the windows. Nicholas admired the beauty for a moment before opening the door to an unfamiliar person: the spy.

"Good day to you, my friend," Nicholas greeted. "Is my help needed?"

"Yes please. It is something that requires Wezenkap," said the spy.

Nicholas placed Wezenkap on his head. Its strength again pulsed through his limbs. "I have my power now," he said.

The spy reached into one of his pockets. "Your greatest challenge is here." He pulled out the bottle and removed the cork.

Nicholas did not expect such action. The spy held the bottle up to the hero's nose. The fumes were strong and his nose began to bleed. It was not the blood that worried Nicholas. The fumes also made his mind dull. Not even the simplest thought could pass through his head. Wezenkap could not save him this time. Nicholas fell into a deep sleep. The spy grinned with wicked pleasure. The dreaded enemy was down! As quickly as he could, the spy grabbed Wezenkap and placed it in his cart. He then grabbed a sheet and placed it over Nicholas's sleeping body. With some effort, the spy placed him in the box and immediately rode off like an undertaker delivering a coffin.

Nicholas was asleep for two full days. He woke to find himself shackled under the night sky, against a palisade wall. His heart sank. Wezenkap was no longer in his reach. Nicholas was helpless. He never thought he would be helpless again. He sat alone in grief when the spy and the goblin captain, both holding lanterns, came up to him. The spy also held Wezenkap. Nicholas's greatest source of power was again in his reach, but now he could not use it. The helmet itself was no longer beautiful. It was spotted with filth and it no longer glistened.

"Sorry you must suffer in this cruel manner," said the captain. "But your helmet is a great threat to my people and we mustn't let you have it."

The spy set down the lantern and placed Wezenkap on his head, much to Nicholas's horror. But the spy did nothing.

"This helmet gives power to no one save you, Nicholas," said the spy.

"And now we must destroy it because of you," the captain finished.

The goblin unshackled Nicholas and tied his arms with a rope. Nearby were to guard towers that flanked the front gates. The captain led Nicholas inside the fort where many goblins and evil dwarves scorned and laughed at him. In the center of the fort was a metal pot filled with molten liquid. The spy gave Wezenkap to the captain, who lifted it high in the air for the viewers to see.

"This is your long-feared object!" he called. "This helmet posed a great threat to us. It gave this dwarf exceedingly great strength!" He pointed at Nicholas. "And now our worries are behind us!"

The captain held Wezenkap over the pot. Nicholas did not bother to fight his way out, for he doubted he had such power. He instead closed his eyes when the captain dropped the great helmet into the molten liquid. A fire erupted from the pot as Wezenkap melted. The tears finally escaped Nicholas's eyes. He was no longer powerful. He was weak. All hope of saving himself was gone. Wezenkap was gone.

The goblin captain ordered Nicholas be locked up until his execution. He was shut up in a small, musty cell within the bowels of the fort. The cell itself was small, even for a dwarf. He sat down against the wall and began murmuring to himself.

"I was nearly killed when Wezenkap was given to me. I did what I could to help others. Now I can't even help myself."

He re-envisioned the moment when he was on the bed where Wezenkap was given to him. Nicholas suddenly stood up when he remembered the fairy's words.

"*I will only use its strength for good,*" he told the fairy.

"*It is your strength from which the helmet draws its power,*" was the fairy's reply.

It was *his* strength. Nicholas's strength. Maybe he could still use Wezenkap's power. There was that possibility!

The thought of it restored faith in Nicholas's heart. With this faith, he grabbed hold of the cell door and pulled as hard as he could. The door bent then ripped from its hinges. Nicholas ran out of his cell and into the courtyard. Several goblins shouted in alarm. Many stood in Nicholas's path to stop him. Nicholas fought off his enemies with his bare hands. Not once was he wounded. His goal was the two guard towers at the gate. He battled his way there. Standing in front of the first tower, he pushed with all his might. The base of the tower groaned. Pushing harder, the entire structure collapsed. The lanterns inside burned the wooden walls and the fire spread throughout the fort before anyone was able to douse it. The entire fort was soon consumed by fire and was no more. Nicholas escaped into the rolling hills. As he ran, he felt his power truly diminish. He had never felt so weak before. He sat down at the top of a hill in the middle of the night. He felt miserable for the loss of Wezenkap, but felt happy that he had destroyed such an evil place. Even with the helmet gone, he continued his good deeds.

The Bell Tower

Once there was an ancient village that sat just outside the Queen's borders. No one lived in this town, for it had been abandoned many years ago. People never visited or even passed through the town, ever since that dreadful night of civil unrest. Before dawn of the following day, hundreds of people in the village had died; the survivors fled with their lives. After the Queen took power, it was believed that the spirits of the dead haunted the streets and houses. Also, in that old town was a cathedral. This was where the most infamous haunting took place. Since the first full moon on the night of the bloody revolt, the cathedral bell had rung precisely at the stroke of twelve. Every full moon thereafter, the citizens of the kingdom expected to hear the distant bell toll. Stories arose that the soul of the long-deceased ringer was responsible. But not everyone was convinced. There were many different theories and answers as to what kind of soul rang the bell. These answers were more opinion than fact, though. The people began arguing and debating with each other. The Queen did not want to upset any of her people, so her opinions remained unknown.

"It could be an evil spirit," one would say to another.

"How can an evil spirit dwell there? A cathedral is a place of God's good, not evil," said another.

Some had different ideas to argue:

"There is no ghost. There's nothing there at all. The ringing is in your mind."

"And do you hear the ringing every full moon?" the contender would ask.

"Sometimes in my mind, but never in my ears, no matter how convincing it sounds. I'm the smartest and that means I'm right."

Organized debates became common. All talk and no listening were the nature of these debates. No one changed their opinion. Pride was an unseen factor. Anger and hatred were in the hearts of most people. If there was a spirit ringing the bell, it was certainly not an evil spirit, for the evil spirit was clearly among many of the citizens of the kingdom.

Amidst the contention was a young woman and her seven-year-old brother. They did not know who to believe. But they knew that no matter what, the truth was still out there, unchanged. The sister and brother were wise enough to know this. They wanted to find out why the bell tolled. They had both heard the bell and knew someone or something was ringing it, ghost or no ghost. It was definitely not in their heads! One day the sister expressed her desire to investigate the abandoned cathedral. This made her brother nervous.

"During the next full moon, we must seek the truth about the bell, Robin," she told her brother one night.

"I've had the same idea, Winifred, but I don't think I want to go. It sounds frightening," said Robin.

Winifred understood Robin's fears. She did not want to force him into something that would frighten him.

"Then the next full moon, I will investigate the cathedral myself. I'll see if this bell-ringer really is a specter. Don't worry, my brother. It may not be as frightening as you think."

Robin was grateful for Winifred's kindness and understanding. They both knew that the next full moon was two weeks away. The next day, Winifred mentioned her idea to the other people of the kingdom. She thought they would be happy with the idea, but was surprised to meet harsh criticism.

"Why investigate the bell tower? It's a ghost, and you should know that," said a stubborn old woman.

"You're a fool! There is nothing there; it is in your mind! Now reason with what is real for a change!" barked a young man.

Winifred did not expect such angry replies. She did not understand why everyone was so hostile. When she found Robin, he was crying. He told her that he had also explained her plan and experienced the antagonistic criticism as well. Winifred was undaunted by the people's words. She prepared for her journey to the abandoned town despite the many dissuasions from the people. On the eve of the next full moon, she packed food, a lantern, and other supplies that are not important for me to list.

"Suppose it *is* a ghost?" Robin told her that night.

"That is for me to discover," said Winifred bravely.

She set off late the next morning. By then a gray mist floated near the ground like a cloud of discouragement. This tested Winifred's bravery. Along the way, a group of worried creatures followed closely behind her. Most were either sheep or goats, but there were two pigs and a mule as well. Moments later, a farmer appeared on the road.

"Are you really going to the old town?" he asked.

"I must go," replied Winifred. "Do you know what will ring the bell tonight?"

The farmer shook his head nervously. The animals seemed ill at ease as well. "I don't. Most definitely I don't," said the farmer. "But what if this specter harms you? You mustn't go. Don't go to the bell tower!"

"I'm on my way to see why the bell rings. I want to find the truth," said Winifred.

The farmer and his animals took a step back; except for a sheep, who took a step forward. It seemed as if it believed visiting the bell tower was a good idea.

"If that is what you want, then take care of yourself and watch for danger," the farmer said at last.

Winifred continued on her way. The farmer offered his mule for Winifred to ride, which Winifred accepted graciously. Several miles up the road, however, the mule stopped at a reasonable distance from the nearest building that was considered part of the old town. He refused to go any further. Winifred secured the mule, gathered her lunch and lantern, then set off on her own. After passing the first house, a bad feeling suddenly washed over her. The feeling was alien. The town was uninhabited, but Winifred did not feel alone. The buildings were weathered, and the trees and what once were shrubs and hedges were overgrown. The thought of so many people being mercilessly slaughtered here triggered enough horror in and of itself. With all the empty streets and buildings, there were many places where someone could hide and spring on an unsuspecting victim.

Winifred felt like she was being watched.

She sat down in a courtyard, slowly eating her lunch when she heard a loud, spontaneous *thump!* followed by a lamenting low. It came from a nearby house! Winifred went to inspect it, but saw no one there. Another sound was heard in the next house. It was another *thump!* as if someone was striking a wall with a club. Winifred did not assume it was a ghost yet, but she did not eliminate that possibility. Even if it was the presence of a mortal being, it still scared her. The wind blew through the window soon after, making a terrible howl that wailed throughout the house. Winifred did not like the noise at all. She immediately left.

All day, strange activity occurred. *Bangs!* and *thumps!* echoed everywhere, yet Winifred could not find any source of the noises. She grew more tense as each hour passed. Every so often a chilling wind would blow through the old town, making a howl that sounded like the cry of a lost wolf pup. Time passed slowly and nightfall finally loomed. The mist blocked the moon's face, but enough light passed through to give the town a faint glow. Winifred lit her lantern. This only offered a dim, flickering light. Shadows moved all around and the howling wind was unsettling to hear. Luckily the random *thumps!* and *creaks!* ceased when the sun set, which made Winifred feel a little better. New worries arose, however, for midnight was approaching.

When Winifred approached the cathedral of long-gone glory, she saw something through a window of the bell tower. It was a light drifting up the staircase. This light was neither candle nor lantern, for it did not flicker.

At first Winifred wanted to run. An invisible hand of ice crawled up her neck, but she could not leave when she was so close to her answer. Something was there!

Plucking up all the courage she could muster, she entered the cathedral. She approached the bottom of the bell tower when the first toll came. The deep sound of the bell began its lonely song. Winifred ran up the stairs that wrapped around the inside of the tower.

The bell tolled again.

She reached the lowest window when her lantern burned out. There was no time to relight it. She kept her hand on the wall so she would not fall on the other side.

The bell tolled again.

Winifred stopped and turned right each time she felt a corner.

The bell tolled again.

She tripped a time or two on the steps. It was easy to lose her balance in the dark. But each time she tripped, she stood right back up and continued.

The bell tolled again.

She reached the window where she had seen the light. She ran right past it.

The bell tolled again.

She finally saw the light at the top. Something was definitely there!

The bell tolled again.

The ringing was much louder the further up she went.

The bell tolled again.

Almost there.

The bell tolled again.

She made it to the top after the exhausting climb. What she saw nearly made her run right back down the tower. The unusual sight was frightening! A bright apparition stood below the rope of the bell. There was no visible hand pulling down on the rope. After a moment, Winifred did not know whether to run or to address the apparition. It took all of her courage and strength to do the latter. Taking a deep breath, she said, "Hello."

Her voice was drowned by the bell's ring. She decided to say it again, only louder.

"Hello!"

The apparition's glow dimmed as it eyed Winifred, who now beheld a hunched figure. It wore a green hood and rags for clothing. It looked like a short man with a long nose. He was quite hideous to say the least. He stared at Winifred until the bell was quiet enough for him to speak.

"How dare you interrupt my monthly ritual! Do you not know what manners are?"

Winifred's fright was not helped by the figure's rude introduction. "I… I beg your pardon. Are you a… ghost?"

The figure put a hand over his heart, as if he was stabbed by a dagger. "A ghost? A ghost? I may be a spirit but I would never call myself a ghost. Hah, ghost!"

Winifred kept her eyes on the spirit. The longer she did, the less fearsome he was. "May I ask why you ring this bell every full moon?" she inquired.

The spirit held a blank expression, which was quite a funny thing to see. He no longer appeared upset. "For peace, child," he said. "This cathedral was once a sanctuary, a place where your fears of the world may be rested. The night of the revolt destroyed all that. I ring the bell on the full moon, for it was a full moon on the night of the revolt. When I ring the bell, my intention is to remind everyone who hears it that there is still peace in this world if we strive to find it."

Winifred was sorry to know that it was the very same bell that caused so much contention among the people in her kingdom. They had to understand that the toll was a sound for peace.

"It is this bell that creates hatred, I'm afraid," said Winifred. She told the spirit about the arguments and debates.

The spirit frowned. "Well, they are blind to what peace is truly about. Hatred was what caused the revolt here."

"And you are not evil, I presume?" asked Winifred.

"Of course I'm not evil!" yelled the spirit, though not out of anger. "This is a church. Evil does not house itself here. What a silly question! I am no angel, but I'm not evil! Did you think I was a demon who was cursed to ring this bell?"

Winifred let out a snicker. She stopped instantly for fear of insulting the spirit, but the spirit took no offense. He laughed too. There was nothing scary about this spirit anymore. He may have sounded fearsome from his yelling, but his laugh added more humor than fright. The spirit rang the bell for peace, nothing more. Now Winifred knew the truth. Nothing could change that. She said goodbye to the spirit after the final, faint toll, and was on her way home early next morning.

As she passed the last house, she rode the mule back to the farm.

"I heard the bell last night! Was it a ghost?" the farmer asked anxiously.

"It was a spirit, a friendly spirit," said Winifred. "There is nothing to fear. It's his job to ring the bell for peace."

The farmer sighed in relief. In gratitude, he offered to lend his mule again, this time for Winifred to go home. Winifred accepted, and she and the farmer went back to the kingdom. When they arrived, the farmer rode off. Winifred first told Robin about her meeting with the spirit. Robin was very happy to hear it. "I did not sleep after midnight when the bell rang," he said. "So, it was not a ghost, but a spirit. With what you've said, I will sleep better during the next full moon. I'm no longer scared. The midnight ring will be a lullaby of peace instead."

As the morning wore on, Winifred told other people about her meeting with the spirit and the message of peace. She was surprised yet again to find that their opinions did not change, unlike the farmer who had trusted her word.

"How dare you say spirit! It was a ghost!"

"You never talk about that again!"

"Don't you ever learn? There is no ghost or spirit or anything like that! It is all in your mind! You should reason like I do, for I know more than you!"

The insults did not hurt Winifred one bit. She knew the truth and they did not. Some people believed her, and that very same spirit spoke to them who had soft hearts. They learned what peace was about and stopped contending with their fellow citizens. The ones who refused to seek the truth said that the spirit's words were not real because they had never heard him themselves. But that particular spirit did not speak to them, for their hearts were hard.

Those who believed never saw the spirit as Winifred had. But they took great comfort every time the moon was full and the bell would ring in the night, telling all who listened that there can be peace.

Wilt & the Witch

There is a path through the woods that branches off the main road. It serves as a shortcut to the nearest village. Only Wilt and his friend have recently used this path. Wilt lived about a mile from the village. In the mornings, he would take the path to where he worked as an apprentice for a blacksmith. He often traveled the path in the morning, but in the evening, Wilt had bad feelings whenever he crossed through the woods. When autumn came and the daylight shortened, Wilt would take the main road home after a long day at the blacksmith's shop.

Early one morning, Wilt took the path through the woods. The trip was looking to be a quick one. But about halfway through the woods, Wilt noticed footprints in the path. They were smooth and triangular-shaped. Wilt did not recognize the prints. Perhaps someone else had discovered the path in the woods? Sometime later, Wilt saw someone approach him from the distance. He assumed it was the person who had made the prints. He felt unsettled when the stranger appeared to be an old hag. She wore a black cloak with a hood over her wispy white hair. Her nose was long and the tip of it was home to a big black wart. In her right hand was a splintered cane. Wilt feared that she could be a witch. If she was, then what an ugly witch she appeared to be!

Despite her nasty looks, Wilt tried to be polite. "Pardon me, ma'am. I don't mean to block your way."

"You have my pardon," said the witch in an oddly sweet tone. "Do you care to visit my home for a cup of tea?"

The proposal caught Wilt by surprise. There was something suspicious about this old hag. "No thank you," he said. "I shouldn't be late. The blacksmith always wants me to be on time."

"Oh, but you must have at least one cup," the hag pleaded. "It will be brief."

"Sorry ma'am, but I can't be late."

He tried to step around the hag when she placed her foot in front of Wilt. An eerie scowl crossed her pale face.

"Please, young man."

With one tap of her cane, a warm wind brushed through the woods. Nearby creatures and other strange beings began gathering round them, as if they saw the hag as their master. The common animals came in various sizes. Some were as small squirrels while bigger animals like a deer and a moose were also present. Bluebirds, hummingbirds, and swallows fluttered over their heads. There were also little fairies and glowing butterflies that left trails of light wherever they flew. After seeing all these creatures, Wilt almost gave in to the witch's proposal; that was until his gaze returned to the old hag. She was clearly a witch! Wilt did not believe the animals and the fairies had any evil intentions against him, but the witch certainly did.

"I'm sorry, but I have to go," he said as he tried to step around the witch again.

The witch had a frown on her face before giving an innocent smile. Wilt only saw two rotten teeth in that smile. "Perhaps later," she replied.

She stepped aside to let Wilt pass. When Wilt was on his way, he did not look back until he was in the village. He arrived just in time for work. He decided not to mention his encounter to the blacksmith. The day went on with no trouble. That evening, however, Wilt took the main road home. He did not meet the witch then, but he did hear an unnerving howl in the distance. Wilt did not know whether the witch was watching him or not, so he returned home as quickly as possible. Wilt did not see the witch the next day, but he again heard the howling. He decided that he should tell his friend about the witch before he took the path again. His friend was a person to trust; Fredrick was his name. He lived in the village, but he had traveled the path before. Wilt told him about his experience during a break from his work. Fredrick admitted that he had also heard the howling. "You may have the day off tomorrow," he said to Wilt. "You should investigate all this."

Wilt believed that that was a good idea. He planned to do just that. Unfortunately, Fredrick would be too busy that day to join him. While Wilt was on his way home that evening, he never thought he would meet anyone on the main road. Then, to his surprise, the moose came from the woods! Wilt was ready to run when the moose said, "Don't be afraid. Why do you not take the path? It's beautiful in the woods!"

Wilt said, "I don't want to take that path tonight."

"But you love the path!" said the moose. "Are you scared of the witch? She is nice, you'll see."

"No thanks," Wilt replied sternly.

The moose said nothing more and left.

Wilt continued on his way when the deer came from the woods. "Why do you not take the path?" the deer said. "It's beautiful in the woods!"

Wilt again said, "I don't want to take that path tonight."

"But you love the path!" exclaimed the deer. "Are you scared of the witch? She is nice, you'll see." The deer bounded off.

The howling came again, this time it was closer! Wilt ran the rest of the way home. Some of the little fairies came along and fluttered over his head. "Oh, please visit the witch! You will like her! She is nice, you'll see!" they called.

Wilt did not respond. He did not say another word until he reached his home. The little fairies let him be once he closed the door. Though the creatures that talked to Wilt were not frightening (except maybe the moose), he wished to be left alone. His parents were gone for the week, and Wilt felt restless that evening. He could not eat his porridge in peace, for another little fairy tapped on the kitchen window. The fairy stood on the windowsill, staring at Wilt with beady hazel eyes, as if it was pleading for Wilt to let it inside. Wilt ignored the fairy's taps. That night, when he was in bed, he saw the butterflies hovering outside his window. As you should have already known, these were no ordinary butterflies. They each emitted a bright green light, almost lighting the inside of the room. Wilt did not sleep well that night. He had had enough. He knew the little fairies and butterflies were trying to persuade him to visit the witch, along with the moose and the deer. He had to confront the witch and put a stop to this, but he knew he should never drink the tea. Fredrick's advice had to be heeded, so Wilt devoted the next day to finding her. He was on his way shortly after dawn, taking the path into the woods. On his way, the little fairy from the previous night followed him. "Are you going to see the witch?" she asked.

"I am," said Wilt.

The fairy continued to follow him for a short while. After that, she flew off into the woods.

Wilt reached the spot where he had first met the witch. There he began his search for her. It was not long before he found a house. It looked old but habited. There was a tiny plume of smoke coming from the chimney. Wilt assumed it was the witch's house. He knocked on the front door. No answer. Wilt cracked open the door. The house was empty, but it looked nice and neat inside. There was a kettle sitting on a rather bare table, and something was bubbling in a cauldron that hung over the fire. There was also a peach basket full of peaches in the back corner. The witch's splintered cane leaned against the wall. As Wilt entered the house, the howling returned. It sounded like it was right outside! Wilt was wondering what he should do when the witch suddenly appeared in the doorway.

"Why, the young prince has finally come! Care for a cup of tea now? It will be nice and hot."

"No thank you," said Wilt. "What is your reason for coming here and wanting me to have your tea?"

"I just want to be kind. Come have a cup. Please, just one." The witch went over to the kettle and poured some tea into a little white cup. She offered it to Wilt. "Just one sip? Don't be rude."

The more desperate the witch became, the more resistant Wilt was. Soon enough, the witch seemed to have realized that Wilt would never accept her tea, so she smashed the cup onto the floor. A dark cloud spewed from the broken cup. Was that even tea to begin with?

Wilt was astonished by the cloud. While he was distracted, the witch grabbed his arms. She was surprisingly strong for her age! "So now you are stubborn, eh? Perhaps you must stay here until you learn your manners," she sneered.

She started dragging Wilt to another room. Wilt remained calm, for he knew not to struggle until he at least had a chance. That chance came when they moved around the corner of the table. The witch briefly softened her grip. Wilt immediately took action and slipped out of her grasp. He hopped on and over the table. He was already at the door before the witch was even halfway around the table. He ran out of the front door and halted... right at the jaws of a snarling wolf! Three others stood behind it. Wilt regretted that he dismissed the source of the howling the way he had. The wolf barked; yellow foam dripped from its mouth. Its eyes were white as snow. If you ask Wilt, he would say it looked rabid. He gave one last glance at the four wolves and then ran along the side of the house. The wolves were immediately after him. Wilt rounded the corner and found a window. In panic, he climbed up on the sill and shattered the window with his elbow. A great pain which he would never forget ran through his arm. In he crawled with the wolf snapping at his feet. Wilt was sure that whatever cuts he got from the broken glass would be nothing compared to being eaten alive by four ferocious wolves. He raced through the room and back into the kitchen where the witch was waiting for him. She held another cup of tea in her hands.

“One sip and my wolves won’t eat you,” she said. “If you don’t, then you will be their late breakfast. Please don’t be foolish, prince.”

Wilt had a quick mind. He grabbed the cup from her hands and smashed it onto the floor, just as the witch had done before. The puff made the witch step back, right into the fireplace! Though she was not burned since her magic protected her, the witch *did* spill whatever was in the cauldron. She cried out in despair. “Yahhhhh! You foolish boy! You will regret that!”

The wolves came into the house, but they had their eyes set on the witch instead of Wilt. They no longer had yellow foam dripping from their mouths. With a shrill bark from each, all but one chased her away. The witch ran off. It was unclear whether she escaped the wolves or not. Anyhow, she was never seen in those woods again.

The last wolf approached Wilt with a wagging tail, then came the deer and the moose and the bluebirds and the magical butterflies and the little fairies. They all appeared grateful. Perhaps whatever was in the cauldron bound the creatures in a spell. They had served the witch, and now they were free. Had Wilt drank the tea, he could have been bound in the same spell.

Each creature gave his or her natural word of “thanks” to Wilt (they seemed to have lost their ability to speak to him directly). The little fairies kissed him on the head and the magical butterflies landed on his hands. When the butterflies fluttered off, Wilt doused the fire. Now that the witch was gone, Wilt took the short path every day, no matter if it was day or night in the woods. He was never alone since the animals and little fairies often greeted him with grateful hearts.

The Unicorn

You may have heard about the castle of St. Cassius. If you haven't, do not worry; you'll learn soon enough. The castle stood many years ago as one of the finest strongholds in all the land. You may wonder how such a place came to be. Well, this story will tell you just that.

Cassius was a priest who lived most of his days in a kingdom now forgotten. He was a good man and was respected by many…

…that was until the dreams came.

One night, Cassius envisioned the destruction of the entire kingdom. Buildings burned, farms were pillaged, and darkness reigned with an armored fist. Not even the King could save himself. Enemies came from across the sea and enslaved those who could not fight. Those who had the courage to fight perished by the sword. The whole dream was purely grim.

Cassius first believed that it was only a nightmare, so he continued his good work the next day without worry. But the very next night, he again dreamed of the destruction of his kingdom. Everything was the same as before. Then came the third night when he had the same dream again. Cassius realized that these were no simple dreams. They were warnings! The kingdom was in danger! When morning came, Cassius set out to warn the people of kingdom. The people, of course, did not want to listen. They believed their kingdom was too powerful to fall, for it was prospering like never before. Cassius begged for them to heed his warning, but the people laughed and scorned him. Some even threw rocks and stones at the old man. Most of the nobles threatened to kill him if he spoke of the dreams any more. His friends now called him a fool.

Almost all respect for Cassius was lost. Almost. He was on his way to the monastery one day when a young man caught up with him. The young man's name was Charles.

"Priest! I must tell you that there is a family who believes your warnings, but their only son is very upset," said Charles. "I believe your words and warnings are true as well."

Cassius nodded, but did not smile. He knew time was short. "Our enemies are on their way. We must leave immediately."

Charles was surprised to hear this. He returned home as soon as possible and began gathering supplies. Leaving was difficult for Charles since was faithful to the crown. If he left with Cassius, he would never come back, even if he wanted to. However, Charles believed Cassius and knew he had to leave. As hard as it was, he only gathered what he needed and not what he wanted. There was no time to lug everything. The invaders could come at any moment, so he had to be quick! He left all the riches and luxuries a nobleman had. He abandoned his furniture, money, and he left his home without looking back, never to see it again. Since he was one of few who listened to Cassius, his future was bright, though it did not seem that way at first. He packed some food and a few tools and rode off to the unknown. Charles soon found Cassius, who was waiting for him and the other family. Charles was on a horse while Cassius rode a mule. The other family arrived not long after Charles. The parents shared a donkey while the son rode his own horse. They led another mule that carried their supplies. The son's head was drooped low in sorrow.

"Are all who are coming present?" asked Cassius when everyone expected had arrived.

"Sadly yes," said the mother of the family.

Cassius bowed his head. "Very well. We shall go now."

They all started on their way. Cassius led the party, for he knew where to go. Off they all went into the wilderness. While they traveled, Charles heard the son muttering to himself.

"How do I know the old priest is right? He could be leading us to nowhere for no reason. He only had dreams after all."

"Sidney, Cassius is a wise priest. He would never lead us astray," said his mother.

"I wish I was home in bed," Sidney griped.

Charles ignored the mutterings. He instead kept his mind forward.

Cassius and his followers traveled well into the night. Everyone was weary, yet they continued until Cassius said they could rest. They tied their beasts and brought out their blankets and mats. They all slept soundly until the last hours of the night. Before the sun was up, however, Charles was awakened by Cassius.

"You must go back to the King's land and find something within the borders of the kingdom," said the old priest.

Charles was baffled at what he had just heard. "Why must I return? We left to escape destruction."

"There are other dangers that lay ahead of us," said Cassius, "but these new dangers can be avoided. I had a dream while I slept. There is something that you must find before we can continue."

"What sort of thing do I need to find?" asked Charles.

"Hair from the mane of a unicorn."

"A unicorn?"

"Precisely. The power of a unicorn will give us the protection we need. Without a piece of its mane, we will perish."

"Can't we use a unicorn's mane to protect ourselves from the destruction of the kingdom?" asked Charles.

"Our future is best in a new land, and a unicorn's protection will help us this way. You and Sidney must leave at dawn. You must hurry before destruction comes upon the kingdom."

When Charles accepted the mission, Cassius gave him some shears. Charles placed them in his satchel. Cassius then woke the family and explained to Sidney what needed to be done: to get the mane of a unicorn. Sidney groaned at the thought of such a task.

"This is important, Sidney," said his father. "You must do this."

Sidney closed his eyes in frustration. "If you think I should, I guess I will go. But where can we find a unicorn within the borders of the King's land? I have never seen a unicorn, and now we must go back and find one? We will be going back to where we started. We were told to leave the kingdom."

Charles began thinking about the task at hand. He knew the mission sounded strange, but he knew Cassius was right. "I understand the nature of this mission," he said to the priest, "but I know you would not send me and Sidney unless you know we could succeed. If you ask me to find the mane of a unicorn, I will do that."

Cassius was pleased with Charles's willingness. He turned to Sidney, who turned away. "I will go if you want me to," Sidney said with a sigh.

Cassius shook his hand. "Thank you, Sidney. The rest of us will wait here until you return. We will not leave without you."

Charles and Sidney had a quick breakfast of bread and cheese before they left. Their mounts were saddled and they were off just as the sun brought forth a new day. Charles brought the satchel that carried the sheers. All through the morning, Sidney complained while constantly rubbing the sleep from his eyes.

"That old priest believes too much in his dreams," he muttered. "He's mad, I say, for making us look for a silly unicorn. He's mad for saying our kingdom will be destroyed to begin with. There is no reason for all of this."

"Have faith," said Charles. "Cassius is a good man. We will find a unicorn soon enough."

"I hope so," Sidney replied angrily.

He and Charles traveled the way they had come. Sidney was constantly upset, but Charles was determined. He trusted Cassius with his life. It was half-past noon when they reached the borders of their soon-doomed kingdom. The King's people were going about their business, giving no heed to the warning for the impending destruction.

"This is no place to find a unicorn. There is no place to find one," Sidney lamented.

"We will find one," said Charles.

They continued onward. Some people saw them and started to laugh. A few mocked their return, believing they were too cowardly to follow the foolish priest.

"The yellows could not survive the wilderness! They came back to face the imaginary raiders!" they hooted.

Charles remained undaunted by the scorning, but Sidney did not. He turned right around and rode off, which made the people laugh even more. Charles was about to follow him when a knight of the great chivalry rode up to him. "You are a noble no more, but a traitor. You must leave now or be arrested," he warned.

Charles said he would leave. He rode away from the knight's sight in search of Sidney. He found the boy dismounted and sulking next to a peasant's field.

"I did not come all this way to be scorned for something I never wanted to do to begin with!" he yelled. "I don't want to find a unicorn. I want to go home!"

"It's too dangerous to return home," said Charles. "When we have what we need, you'll feel better. I promise."

Sidney remained silent for a moment, then he stood up. "We will see soon enough. I don't want to be scorned, so I will search these fields."

"Very well." Charles did not expect to find a unicorn in the fields. He believed Sidney simply did not want to search.

They rested for a few minutes before continuing. Sidney searched the perimeter of the fields in a very slow manner. Charles, on the other hand, looked in many different hollows and meadows. Even in places where unicorns were thought to prosper were only inhabited by the common woodland creatures. At least Charles noticed that Sidney's mood was improving when they took another brief break a few hours later. They both searched until dusk came, and still there was no sign of a unicorn. There was no place that seemed possible for such a magical creature to roam. Even Charles was becoming discouraged! He met up with Sidney, who was again dismounted and sitting on the ground.

"The night draws nigh and there is no place to sleep," he murmured. "We'll not find housing since we are exiled. This was truly a foolish mission. This land is no place for a unicorn. Why a unicorn? Why? The people will think I'm mad because I thought my house would get robbed and now I come back to look for a prancing unicorn because its mane will protect me."

Charles was at a loss of words. He did not know what to say to comfort the angry Sidney. He silently gazed up at the sky. A clear full moon bathed the land in its mystic light. Charles was becoming upset as well.

"I can't imagine a creature like a unicorn roaming here either," he whispered so Sidney would not hear. "It must be here or else Cassius would never send us back. It must-"

Charles stopped talking. Off in the field, he saw the faint image of something white and graceful. It ran freely in the distance near a peasant's house. He thought his eyes were deceiving him at first. He blinked a few times. Sure enough, something was there. Charles dismounted his horse and slowly approached whatever was out there. As hard to believe as it was, it looked like a white stallion, except there was a long, spiraling horn on its head. A horn! They had found a unicorn after all this time! Charles felt bad that he thought Sidney was foolish for searching the fields. The unicorn was indeed in the fields, not in the hollow nor the meadow.

Sidney saw it too. "Quite a place to see a unicorn," he said. From the tone in his voice, he seemed to believe that searching the fields was foolish as well. His mood also seemed to have suddenly changed.

"No matter its location, we found it! Cassius knew it would be here!" Charles was excited, but he tried to stay as quiet as possible.

The unicorn was nibbling on a cabbage crop as Charles approached it. He pulled another cabbage plant from the ground and held it out in his hand. He continued forward until he was about ten feet away from the majestic beast. The unicorn lifted its head. When its eyes met his, a strange feeling came over Charles.

The beast's eyes almost looked like fire. Its horn glistened in the moonlight, but Charles was focused on its long mane that waved like a flowing sheet of snow. It was indeed a beautiful creature, and it was the key for protection in the new land.

Sidney did not move from his spot. He did not want to spook it. Charles slowly made his way to the unicorn with the cabbage in his hand. He then pulled out the sheers from his satchel. He walked right up to the unicorn and stroked its neck. Its coat was very soft. The unicorn huffed, but it did not run. Instead, it started munching on the cabbage in Charles's hand. With a single swift snip, a small patch of its mane fell to the ground. The sudden snip caused the unicorn to jump. It reared, causing Charles to fall backwards, then whinnied an enchanting whinny and galloped off in a flash.

The unicorn was there, and then it was gone. The meeting was very brief. Charles was not hurt, but rather stunned. He got back to his feet, his legs shaking. He quickly picked up the hair from off the ground. It seemed to be emitting a light of its own. Perhaps it was a reflection of the moonlight. When Sidney came, Charles showed him the hair.

Sidney smiled. "I'm sorry I have ever doubted you, Charles, or Cassius."

"You are brave for coming with me, Sidney. Thank you."

As Charles placed his sheers and the hair in his satchel, the door to the peasant's house opened. A man came running out. "What was that in my field?" he cried. He already seemed to know the answer, for he had an expression of awe.

"What we found was a miracle," said Charles.

"A true miracle indeed, my good noble," said the peasant. "Having a beast like that in my field is a strange enough occasion. But how did you touch it? Unicorns are never fond of menfolk like you or me. They will run if they even suspect our presence. You, however, walked right up to it and sheared off a part of its mane. Telling someone of this will make you sound like a novice liar. But you *did* touch it! That is the miracle you are speaking of!"

Sidney explained to the peasant why they had sought the unicorn, and about the upcoming destruction of the kingdom. He invited the peasant to come with him and Charles. The peasant did not make an immediate decision, as expected. He stared at Charles's satchel, not saying anything for an entire minute. Then he asked, "How can a priest build a new kingdom with just a few followers?"

"There will be a way," said Sidney. "We never expected to see a unicorn in your fields. You never expected Charles to even touch the unicorn. Cassius will only tell us to do the possible. There will be a way."

Charles was pleased with Sidney's faith. The boy's attitude had clearly changed since seeing the unicorn. The peasant and his wife joined Charles and Sidney on their journey back into the wilderness. They reached Cassius's party the next day. All rejoiced at the reunion.

The mane of the unicorn truly did protect Cassius's people. Now you may ask yourself how a priest and his six followers could have possibly founded such a kingdom that gave rise to the mighty castle. Well, as a matter of fact, Sidney was right. Cassius did not assign anything to anyone unless there was a way to accomplish it. The raiders did indeed attack several kingdoms, and the refugees who heeded the warnings of the wise found the place where Cassius's people settled. Years passed and the people prospered. Soon enough, the great castle was built in honor of the founding priest. St. Cassius Castle became a symbol of faith and peace.

Many years later, some people will tell you that sometimes at night, a white steed with a long, spiraled horn and a flowing mane will run by the castle walls. Those who say they have seen it say that St. Cassius Castle is protected. They say St. Cassius will always stand as long as the unicorn runs free.

Thief & Victim

There was once a farmer who always worked very hard. Every year he made sure that his farm was the best that it could be, no matter what challenge nature brought his way. One autumn day the farmer was inspecting his corn field. The weather had been merciless the year before due to the many windstorms. This sadly brought a low crop yield. Luckily the recent spring promised a better year. The farmer was looking forward to seeing good, healthy crops. But when he laid his eyes upon his precious corn, a feeling of hatred struck his heart. Two stalks were down and all the ears on those stalks were gone!

The farmer knew the cause of such damage without a doubt. He had dealt with this problem before. Raccoons. Filthy, ravaging raccoons! The farmer hated raccoons more than anything. He hated them more than he hated wolves, rats, rabbits, foxes, or even pesky beetles. Raccoons have always been a nuisance. They always stole his corn without a second thought. Raccoons were thieves, and the farmer knew all about it. On that autumn day, he swore a bitter vengeance that he would find this thief and bring proper justice to it.

"This pest has got to go," he growled. With only two stalks down, he knew there was only one he had to deal with.

And so, the hunt for the robbing beast began. The farmer set up all sorts of traps in and around his corn fields. Certainly, raccoons were not smart enough to avoid *his* traps! He sent his workers out among the farmlands to hopefully find and get rid of the raccoon. The farmer had a sense of peace for the rest of the day, knowing that his property was safe.

He had a good breakfast the next morning. He ate quickly because he wanted to check his traps as soon as possible. While on his way, he met one of his workers. "Did you find the raccoon?" the farmer asked.

"No," said the worker, "but it was here last night. Some of your traps have been sprung."

The farmer threw his hat down on the muddy ground and stomped on it in anger. "That little devil has seen the last of its days for stealing what's rightfully mine! I want it dead by tomorrow!"

The farmer's fiery hatred against raccoons grew immensely. He believed they were purely evil, and their lives were devoted to thievery. They did not live honest lives like menfolk did. Why must this civilized farmer fall victim to these savage creatures?

His bad temper slowly subsided as the day moved on. The farm was actually looking much better than it had the year before. Even the corn, ready to be harvested in a few weeks, was doing very well (save the stalks destroyed by the raccoon's paws, of course). There were not that many stalks that were harmed, though. They were just a few out of several fields. The farmer was not worried that he would lose all his corn, he just did not want to admit that a raccoon could outwit him. The farmer was a prideful man. He thought his workers were going to take care of the raccoon soon, which made him feel a little better that night.

The next morning came. The farmer left early for the corn fields again. He believed the terror had ended. But as he inspected his field, he found two more earless stalks down. All sense of peace vanished. In the mud, he found a trail of footprints. The hind feet were long and skinny while the front looked like little hand prints. The farmer stomped over the tracks. He was ready to take matters into his own hands. That very day, he acquired a dog. The only kind available was a Labrador. It may not have been a bloodhound, but it was better than nothing.

The dog did his best, but it was not good enough. The raccoon still came despite the dog and the traps. It was never caught. After a while, work on the farm slowed. The farmer became obsessed with the raccoon so much that he could not get his mind off it. He hated the fact that an animal kept outwitting him. A few days later, he purchased newer and crueler traps. He planned to spend the night outside by his field. When the raccoon came, he was going to give it its proper punishment. The weapon he planned to use was a knife. No, a knife was too quick a punishment. A stone! Yes, a stone would be the perfect tool to bring such a menace to justice!

Everything was ready by dusk. The traps were set, and the farmer had a blanket, a lantern, and a big stone. Using a stone brought the risk of scratch and bite wounds if the raccoon fought back, but the stone would bring its justice no matter what. Now the beast was going to learn the penalty for stealing from honest, civilized people.

It was cold that night, so the farmer bundled up in his blanket. The dog was not with him because the farmer was determined to take care of this himself.

An hour had gone by and the farmer was about to fall asleep… then it came! He heard the sound of rustling corn stalks, and then the cry of an ensnared raccoon! It was a sound that was both great and terrible, satisfying yet frightening. The cry pierced the farmer's ears as he lit the lantern and grabbed the stone. His chance had finally come! He was ready for the thief to fight back until its inevitable finish.

There it was, staring back at him with dark eyes. A chain kept its injured foot tethered to a wooden stake.

The farmer set the lantern on the ground and lifted the stone high in the air. His pride had indeed returned. The stone was about to come down upon the raccoon's head when it suddenly cried, "Please don't!"

The farmer froze with the stone over his head. Did the raccoon just speak to him? It couldn't have. The farmer and the animal stared at each other. The raccoon neither hissed nor bared its teeth. It made another cry, then said, "I never intended to cause trouble, I didn't. Please let me go. This snare is hurting my foot."

The raccoon pulled on its leg that was caught in the trap. The chain clanked as it bounced. As shocked as the farmer was, he did not want to lose his newly-restored pride. The stone remained high in the air.

"You may have not intended harm, you thief, but you have caused harm. This corn is not yours. It's mine! When it's harvested, it will go to the markets where it will provide food to honest people for the winter. You wouldn't understand our way of life."

"I understand why this food is here, I really do," said the raccoon. "The food on this farm is yours, I know. I understand you grow it for others."

The farmer did not expect the raccoon to say such things. He lowered the stone slightly, but then lifted it high again. "If you know all that, then why do you steal from me?"

"I do not steal. I, like you, must have food to survive. Have you ever suffered for days with no food, only to find that your only meal lies in danger's way? I have. Life is not easy for me."

The farmer did not lower the stone an inch. His anger overcame him. "The food I grow is for people, not filthy raccoons like yourself! You're a pest. Humans are superior. All you do is eat, sleep, and do whatever your instinct tells you to do. You can't think and reason like I can. Now I must protect my farm! I am civilized and this is what I must do!"

He was ready to beat down the raccoon when it suddenly hissed and jumped forward, biting his ankle and snarling in an aggressive manner. This was the typical aggression expected of a raccoon. The startled farmer stumbled back, nearly kicking over the lantern. The stone slipped from his fingers and landed on his foot. He cried out with tears running down his face. The raccoon took a step closer to him. It would have been closer had it not been restrained by the trap.

"If I was not able to speak to you, I'd fight you," it said. "You would then finish the whole confrontation with that stone. You call yourself civilized? Look at you, criticizing my instincts while yours make you cruel and savage. I'm a living thing just like you. I follow my own instincts and think and make choices like you. Think about what you're doing! If you're truly superior as a human being, then you have a responsibility to carry."

The farmer was about to pick up the stone when he looked back down at the raccoon. Even after all it had done, it stared at him with a steady gaze. The bite on his ankle was not a serious wound. He was not even bleeding. What hurt more was his heart. He realized that the raccoon understood everything. It was *he* who did not understand! The raccoon was not the thief, it was the victim! All pride inside the farmer crumbled. He dropped to his knees in deep sorrow.

"I know you are troubled, I do," the raccoon continued. "It's not cruel in any way to defend your corn. You have a right to do that, as it is your property after all. I know this as well. But you must remember that I do not seek to steal. I only seek food. Can you understand that?"

The farmer lumbered to his feet, but left the stone in the soil. He took a deep breath. He knew now that the raccoon was no thief at all. It was only trying to find food. What was so savage about that? The farmer began to understand. Now he wondered how he could help the raccoon while keeping his farm running the way it should. "I have an idea," he said, calming himself. "My crops must be harvested. I cannot let them be consumed freely, for I will lose money and later the whole farm. I need the profit. Perhaps I can offer a small portion of corn to you?"

"You must know that I will soon become a mother," said the raccoon.

The farmer almost succumbed to frustration, but he took another deep breath. "I see. Do you accept my offer then?"

"I accept," the raccoon answered graciously.

With everything the farmer learned that evening, the raccoon had also learned many things. She learned to only take what was allowed. The farmer set her free and addressed her leg. From that time forth the farmer continued a successful harvest.

The next year was dry. Times were difficult on the farm during dry spells. The farmer continued what he did to protect his crops, but he no longer hated the animals who tried to take his food. The raccoon had her small share of corn that fed her family. That share of food also fed other animals who were looking for it. They first fought amongst one another, but they also had to understand that everyone else was simply trying to survive. The farmer and the raccoon shared what they had, and the fighting soon stopped. The farmer was generous to all. He understood. To the raccoon he once hated, he was now a friend.

Rollins

Harold was in grief. The two spoiled girls would not stop fighting. These fights were more verbal than physical, but they were just as upsetting to watch. These girls, Ruben and Merilen, often spent the day at old Harold's home while their parents were away. Nobody else wanted to mind them or their fighting, so the burden lay on Harold's shoulders. Every time Ruben and Merilen were in his home, they argued and yelled at each other at every possible second. One day, their parents left and would not be back until the next evening. Harold, exhausted as he was, promised to mind them. He was going about his other businesses that night when he heard a loud crash that came from the outer room. He arrived to find the two girls staring at a pile of broken shards on the floor. Neither of them looked ashamed, but rather dumbstruck.

There it was again: a typical, disgusting display by these reckless girls! And they had the audacity to do such a thing without a glint of guilt! The shards were from a china vase that Harold's mother had given to him many years ago. Harold almost mourned for the loss of such a memento.

"Who broke this vase?" he asked harshly.

Ruben and Merilen both pointed at each other. "She did it," they said in unison.

Harold became more upset. It was both their faults that the vase broke. "You will both go to bed right this minute!" he ordered. "What happened is inexcusable."

"But it wasn't my fault!" cried Ruben.

"Yes it was," said Merilen, still pointing at her.

Harold pounded his cane against the floor. "You will both go to bed now!" He pointed to their bedroom.

The girls did as they were told and retired to their room. Now if you expect that they were going to fight rather than sleep, then you're right. Harold could hardly sleep himself because of it. Listening to them bicker over the most ridiculous things was a true bother. That was the tipping point for Harold. That night, he made up his mind to show his secret to the girls and teach them the good things of peace. The next morning, the girls moaned and wailed for their breakfast.

"You won't get your breakfast until after I show you something," said Harold. "Your fighting and arguing must stop."

"But I'm hungry!" wailed Merilen.

"It's your fault we can't have our breakfast," said Ruben.

"It's not my fault!"

Harold slammed his hand on the table before the new fire kindled. "Enough! Now get your shoes and follow me."

The girls were very upset. But they knew if they wanted their breakfast, they had to obey. Harold grabbed his cane and did not allow the girls to say a single word. He led them outside and into the forest. The girls became worried.

"Why are you taking us out here?" Ruben asked nervously.

"I told you, no talking," said Harold, firm in his command.

Ruben and Merilen miraculously remained quiet. Harold, knowing his way, came to a well-worn path. He led the girls deep into the forest. They ventured deeper and deeper for the rest of the morning until they came to a small pond. Harold stopped here, not even the least bit fatigued. Though the pond was small, it looked rather deep; and despite being in the heart of the forest, there was only one tree at its bank: a large fir. This fir stood out among the rest of the trees, and not just because of its location. It had a bright and mysterious appearance as well. On its upper branches sat a mighty hawk, staring down at the company that had just arrived. A single glance would tell you that this fir stood for a special reason.

The girls did not know what that reason was yet. They were to find out soon enough.

"Why have you brought us here?" Merilen asked.

"Your fighting is most disgraceful and wrong," Harold said. "This place in the forest holds peace. It is all stored in this mighty fir and quiet pond. There is no contention of any sort here. What you are about to see will hopefully change your ways."

The girls did not see anything particular at first, but then something came from the cover the woods. It trotted up to the pond and took a drink. It was a unicorn! Its long, swirling horn glimmered in the sunlight as if it was made of icy diamond, and its coat was pure white. The girls were shocked yet amazed. Save the singing of birds, all was silent near the pond. That was so until the fir at the pond's edge trembled and shook. The hawk swooped down from its branches and nestled on the ground beside tree. The girls were afraid at first. The tree twisted and turned until the bark on its trunk resembled the face of a man.

"Fear not children. Though I move, I have not fallen.
You see me as a tree, and my name is Rollins."

The fir's voice was deep and gentle. The needles on its branches shook like flags as it spoke. Upon hearing his voice, the unicorn lifted its head, bowed in respect to Rollins, and moved to the other end of the pond to drink.

"O, great Rollins," said Harold to the fir. "These young lasses are quarrelsome and bitter. Tell them of peace, which you hold so dear."

"We are not quarrelsome and bitter," Ruben protested.

The fir waved its lower branches.

"But you are; and if you don't learn,
You will always be at War.
Through Peace there are rewards to earn
That Pride has no room to store."

What Rollins had said caught Merilen's attention first. "What kind of rewards are these?" she asked.

"These are not material rewards that mortal people covet," said Harold.

"Precisely," replied Rollins,

> *"Hearken, and view the forest 'round you,*
> *For only Peace dwells here.*
> *See the pond and in its depths of blue,*
> *The rewards of Peace are clear."*

The girls turned their attention once again to the wonderful unicorn. Other creatures came to the pond as well. There were things they recognized: elk, reindeer, and sparrows; and there were things they did not recognize: three little fairies and, of course, the unicorn.

Harold pointed at each being. "These creatures all have peace. Never do they argue or fight. They will only come to you if you have peace as well."

"See the pond in its depths of blue," the fir repeated.

Ruben and Merilen peeked in the clear water. They saw mermaids swimming about. They had such beautiful tails, with colors that ranged from blue to green, yellow to violet, and red to orange. The mermaids smiled when they saw Ruben and Merilen, not one of them frowned. This pond in the forest was truly a wonderful place! Harold knew that peace would always be in the forest as long as Rollins was here. He hoped now that the girls might see the peace of the fir as well. Merilen patted the elk and reindeer, and the sparrows landed on Ruben's shoulders and sang sweet songs.

Everyone stayed all through the afternoon. The girls, forgetting their breakfast, did not want to leave. Not once did they raise their voices against each other. They were silent all day.

Eventually, the beings of the forest left. The hawk flew back to the top of the fir's branches. The three fairies waved and blew kisses before they fluttered away. The elk, the reindeer, and the sparrows left soon after. When the mermaids disappeared into the depths of the pond, the girls were sorry to see them go. The unicorn, the last one there, finally trotted off. Ruben and Merilen stared at the tree's reflection in the pond. Rollins and the hawk were the only beings who did not leave.

The great fir said,

> *"Perhaps now you'll know that fighting is wrong,*
> *It only brings sorrow and hate.*
> *Never again ring the warring gong,*
> *And see what you can create."*

Ruben and Merilen agreed to that.

"I promise to never fight again," said Merilen.

"Me too," added Ruben.

Rollins made a deep rumble of satisfaction, then he twisted and turned once again. His face was no longer visible, but what he stood for shone brightly in his countenance. The hawk remained in the upper branches; he was guardian of the great fir.

The girls talked about the pond, the creatures, and Rollins the fir for the rest of the day. They returned to their homes as friends. The next time they were at Harold's home, they worked and played together without fuss. This continued on for days. Harold took great comfort knowing that Rollins had brought good virtues to the girls.

Sadly, the good virtues did not last. Several days later, Merilen began boasting that the mermaids were happy because of her. It did not seem like trouble at first, for Ruben took the statement well (even though she didn't believe it one bit). Later, Ruben said that there was peace in the forest because of her. Harold became worried. If the girls were boasting, then the arguing could return. He tried to warn the girls. They said they remembered how wonderful the forest was, but not once did they mention the peace they felt, or Rollins for that matter. They continued to boast.

As Harold feared, the arguing returned. It was worse than ever. They argued about experiences in the forest which were not true. They argued about who was most humble, ironically. The arguing worsened to the point where violence took its despairing place. There was no stopping it. The violent fighting became so bad that the girls could no longer stay at Harold's home. Harold was alone, again grieved. It was such an awful downfall. The saplings the girls had planted were in hard hearts, and therefore were unable to grow.

FREE GRØLS

ONCE UPON A TIME, ON THE WORLD OF ELSOV, THERE WAS a group of little people called grøls. These people live hard lives. Their villages were often captured by monsters such as goblins and ogres. There was one particular village that had been captured several decades before. Several generations of unfortunate grøls were forced to work for the benefit of a group of goblins. After enduring many days of hard work and little rest, the strongest of the grøls sorely wished for freedom. He started making plans to fight his captors. The other grøls were scared to fight when they first heard of the strong grøl's plan. It took their deep hunger for freedom to convince them.

The goblins often forced the grøls from one workplace to another by having them march in lines, two abreast. These marches were always long and exhausting. The strongest grøl led the line with two goblins beside him. The entire line of grøls was silent. The goblins were talking and joking with themselves while occasionally jabbing the butts of their spears at the backs of slower slaves to hurry them on.

Those were the common sounds. Everyone was used them. The strongest grøl was about to carry out his plan when… *snap*! The goblins looked up in the trees by the path. A small army of nymphs jumped out from the branches. The goblins fought back when the nymphs attacked, but the nymphs overwhelmed the goblins and drove them away. When the captors were out of sight, the nymphs unshackled the startled grøls.

"We have driven your enemies out. You are now free," the nymphs announced.

The grøls rejoiced and thanked the nymphs hundreds of times over. Since they were now free, they returned to their village and had a grand celebration. They sang, danced, and had a fine feast. The strongest grøl was the only one who did not join in the revelry. He enjoyed being free, no doubt, but he was upset that he was unable to carry out his plan before the nymphs came. There was something else besides freedom that he lusted for. Another idea came as he listened to the grøls' merriment. They had not yet mentioned the need to establish a new form of government. There was no way they could live in peace without some sort of leadership, and the strongest grøl knew that.

The moment the merriment died down, the strongest grøl proposed himself to be the new king. No one else wanted to contest that, so the strongest grøl became their supreme ruler. A few other grøls liked that idea. The strongest grøl was pleased with this, so he made them his personal guards.

It seemed like a good idea at first. The new King assigned reasonable work to the right people. There was good work and plenty of time to rest. After about a month or so, however, the grøls in the village noticed that their King began to change. He assigned work for his own pleasure, he lived in the biggest tree in the village, he forced some grøls to be his personal chefs and cleaners, and he never did what the other grøls wanted. He only assigned them to do what he wanted.

More time passed and the troubles worsened. The inferior grøls pleaded for their ruler to listen to their words and opinions, but the King scolded them. Those who asked for him to listen were punished with more work and less rest. The King started to do this with all the grøls, save his loyal guards.

It was not long before the grøls found themselves as slaves once again. Their King, a real tyrant, and his guards had no better souls than those of the goblins who had enslaved them before. The strongest grøl no longer wished for freedom; he wished for more power, so he took the freedom from his own people. His power led him to corruption. He may have stopped wishing for freedom, but he was not free. Even though he was the King, he was enslaved by his own pride.

Did the grøls live as slaves for the rest of their lives, or is there a glimmer of hope? That question is yet to be answered.

THE LONG WEEK

BEFORE WE BEGIN ON THIS STORY, I SHOULD FIRST TELL YOU that it is true. It happened to me about three years ago, but I remember it as if it was yesterday. I will never forget that week for as long as I live. My wife took my daughter to a nationwide spelling bee; they left Monday and would not return until the next Sunday. I volunteered to stay home and mind the garden and animals. I didn't think much would happen.

They left early that Monday morning. Once they were gone, I had a quick breakfast of bacon and eggs, then I set off doing the daily chores. The first thing I did was clean the house.

Here is where they came.

After sweeping the kitchen, there was a faint knock on the door, as if a child was doing the knocking. I opened the door to find a little green man grinning maniacally at me. I had never seen one up to this point, but I knew for sure this was a baby troll, and baby trolls can mean a lot of trouble!

"Can I help you?" I asked reluctantly.

"We wish for housing," he said. "Give us your house to stay in and we will all be happy."

I did not expect such a request, nor was I in the mood to comply. Instead of saying no, I foolishly asked, "How long are you going to stay?"

"As long as we wish," was the reply.

The way the baby troll grinned at me made me tremble on the inside. What if I refused? Would he do something horrible?

"Very well," I said. "You can stay for one night, but for one night only."

The little troll squealed. "Yay! Come on in, everyone!"

Before I knew it, dozens upon dozens of the little wretches came flooding in like an army of gnats. It was an awful sight! Everything I had done that morning was undone in a minute. Mud was tracked all over the floor, water from the kitchen sink spilled everywhere, and the beds and tables and chairs were overturned. Some even smashed my wife's favorite pots and pans! Every one of them laughed and chortled to their hearts' content. My wife was not going to be happy to see such a nasty mess. I myself could no longer bear it. I stamped my foot and pointed to the door. All the trolls suddenly stopped and stared at me.

"Enough is enough!" I yelled. "I cannot accept such behavior! You must all leave immediately!"

The little trolls were struck dumb at my outburst. Then, one by one, they crossly walked out the door single file.

"You will regret refusing our demands," said the first troll I had met. "We will seek revenge. Mark my words on behalf of all of us, we will seek revenge." Then he ran off.

I was worried upon hearing that. But once they were gone, I tried not to think about his threat. My new focus was to clean up the mess they had made. It took all the rest of the morning and afternoon. I wasn't able to do my other chores, except for milking the cow, until late that evening. Luckily, the baby trolls did not return then. I had a quick supper and went to bed early, ready to make up for Monday's loss. Tuesday brought a bright, sunny morning. I expected this day to be normal. It started off that way too, until I went to milk the cow again. For an unknown reason, the cow began acting up. She kicked and protested every time I went near her. She had never done that before. Why was she behaving like this now? Could it be the trolls' doing? I hoped not. It took much effort, but I soon milked her. As I started on my way out of the barn with a pail of milk, I heard the sound of squealing pigs and bleating sheep. When I stepped out of the barn, I noticed that they had all escaped! It would be impossible to herd them all back in the pen alone. I tried my best, but to no avail. Then I heard the sound of giggling trolls round the house. There was no question that they were responsible for the animals escaping. For about an hour, I herded about half the pigs and half the sheep back into the pen. The rest of them escaped into the woods.

I hoped that that was the last misfortune of the day, but I was wrong. Feeling upset, I decided to go hunting in the woods. I lowered my rifle from its stand above the mantle and loaded it, then I set off looking for a pheasant or a deer or some other game. As I made my way through the woods, I continued to hear giggling all around me. I hoped they would not upset the beasts I was hunting. Eventually, I found a deer grazing in a meadow. It was the perfect target. I crouched, aimed, and prepared to fire. When I squeezed the trigger, my weapon suddenly exploded into a cloud of smoke. The rifle, which I had inherited from my grandfather, fell into several pieces. The giggling and laughing was now louder than ever before.

"You are still not welcome in my house!" I yelled.

Silence fell, which made me glad. I picked up the pieces of the rifle and returned home with no meat for supper. That night, all I had was a bland bowl of porridge. I was never one to like it. Ever since I was a little boy, I dreaded porridge night. That is still true today. But on that night, porridge was the only thing available for supper. I tried to go to bed early again that evening, but I kept hearing unsettling noises. From my room, I heard doors slam shut and windows opening and closing. When I went to check, there was no one there. I went back to my room only to hear it start all over again. It continued on till about midnight.

The trials of Wednesday started early in the morning. I went out to fetch a bucket of water from the well. But as I hoisted up the bucket, the water looked more like sludge. I sniffed it and immediately turned my head away with a wince. This water was no good; it was poisoned! How dare the trolls! I had no clean water! Throwing the bucket down the well, I went back to the house. I suppose I must use up yesterday's milk to make today's porridge, I thought. I opened the door to grab the ingredients. I withdrew my hand in an instant. Rats! There were rats in the cupboards, liberally munching on all the food I had! Disgusting! If I was to have breakfast, I would have to go to the market. I hitched the mule to my cart and set off down the road. I bought some extra rations (and rat traps) then set off for home. I couldn't help but hear the trolls in the woods giggling again. I looked around, but there were none to be found. When I reached my house, I unhitched the mule. Just as I did so, the mule shrieked and ran off in fright.

"Stop it, you trolls!" I shouted.

No giggling came after my yell. I must have frightened them off. In fact, I was able to go about the rest of the day with no trouble. I thought the night would be like that too. At first it looked like it would. I ate my supper in peace and went to bed. *Crash*! Just before I shut my eyes, a startling noise came from the kitchen. The sound made me jump from my bed. I landed on the floor with a thump! I went out into the kitchen to see what had happened. The window that looked out into the woods had shattered. Now I was getting worried. A cold wind blew through the open window. The best I could do that night was to cover it up with a quilt.

It was on Thursday when my misfortunes started threatening my life. Having repaired my rifle, I decided to try my luck at hunting again. I returned to the same meadow as before, looking for worthy game. The meadow was at the bottom of a steep hill. I kept my eye out for the baby trolls, for I could hear them. But I did not pay attention to the boulder on top of the hill. After hearing more giggling, I went looking for trolls instead. I was halfway up the hill when the trolls found me in the perfect spot. I heard the crashing before I saw the boulder come tumbling down. I had only seconds to jump out of the way, and I took those precious seconds. The boulder missed me by inches. When my senses cleared, I realized that my life was in danger! The trolls could harm me! I ran back home as fast as I could. Once I made it, I ran inside and locked the door. To my horror, the house was again in a mess, this time worse than before! I figured that I had very little time. I locked all the other doors and windows before setting to work on the house. Sometimes I felt tempted to peek out the broken window and see what was outside. When I did, I covered the opening with the quilt as fast as I could. My house was surrounded by baby trolls! Babies they were, but that did not make them any less dangerous. Like snakes, they could be even more dangerous! It was well into the night when I finished cleaning the house. I was not hungry, but I was quite thirsty. All I had to drink was today's milk, which luckily did not spill or spoil along with the rest of the milk we had. Throughout that night, I heard rapping on the front door. I didn't dare open it. All night the rapping continued, and I could not sleep through the noise. The night was long, loud, and unsettling.

Friday morning came in a gradual tease. By the time the sun was up, the rapping stopped. I unlocked the door and cracked it open. Nobody was out there, but I doubted they were gone. When I inspected the barn, I found the cow dead; the sheep and pigs gone. I couldn't bear it any longer. With no sleep last night, and all our livestock gone, I began to feel myself going half-crazy. I went to the tool shed. Everything was gone in there too! I didn't know what to do. I went about the yard, checking and rechecking everything as to what the trolls may have done. Presently, my neighbor, Mr. Coleman, came to my yard.

"Hello!" he called. "I understand you're here alone for the week. How goes it?"

I was too far out of my mind to answer. I ignored him and continued looking around.

Mr. Coleman grew serious. "Your eyes are red and your hair is disheveled. Has something gone wrong?"

Finding no trolls, I felt it necessary to answer my neighbor. "You've got to help me," I said. "They won't leave me alone!"

"Who won't leave you alone?" asked Mr. Coleman.

"The trolls!" I cried. "The baby trolls! They took my animals and they nearly killed me out in the woods. Oh, what can a man do?"

"Surely you must be mistaken," said Mr. Coleman. "Trolls? I've never heard such nonsense."

"Nonsense it isn't," I replied with trembling hands. "They're everywhere. They ravaged my house like wolves, they damaged my grandfather's rifle like vandals, and they nearly crushed me with a boulder like a bunch of ruthless savages!"

Mr. Coleman was at a loss of words. He started walking away.

"Please don't go!" I cried. "I need your help!"

"Sorry, but I'm not sure I believe that baby trolls are bothering you. I think you need more sleep. Goodbye."

I would have pleaded with him more, but my mind was full. All that day, I knew the trolls were watching me suffer. There was little I could do about that. When night came, things took a turn for the worse. More windows were shattered, dishes flung themselves out of the cupboard, the rats returned and finished all my food, and the door sounded as if it was going to be blown over. Again, I did not get any sleep.

It was now Saturday, and I was not looking forward to Sunday. I did not want my family to come home and see me in such a condition. If I wanted this to end, I had to end it myself. That's it! I had to remove the baby trolls by force! But how? I could barely catch a glimpse of them, and they were tormenting me that way. But something still had to be done. I grabbed my grandfather's rifle and threw the door open. That was when I discovered just how dangerous these baby trolls were. There were about a dozen of them standing behind an angry black bear! When the bear saw me, it charged. I had not yet loaded the rifle, so the next best thing I could to was to run back inside. The bear stopped at the door. It didn't try to break in, but it sat there waiting for me.

"Give us housing!" the trolls demanded. "And the bear will not eat you!"

"No!" I yelled back. "You can do whatever with me, but you will never come inside this house! It's mine!"

The bear stayed at the door all day, leaving at dusk. But that was only because a mighty storm came over the woods. Lightning flashed in the dark sky, followed by furious thunder. Rain and hail pelted down like falling walnuts. It did not bother the trolls, for they were laughing and dancing out in the wet yard. For the third straight night, I did not get any sleep.

The storm passed by Sunday morning. This was my last chance to get rid of the naughty trolls. All night they danced and sang, and they continued to do so all morning. My family was coming home soon, which meant I had to act quickly. I opened the door, holding my loaded rifle. The trolls all stopped and stared at me.

"You have had enough of our games, we presume," they said. "Perhaps you will satisfy our demands now?"

"I wish to go to church today, but I can't with you here," I replied. "This is the last I will deal with you. The next one who demands housing here will receive a bullet."

The trolls did not giggle after that. This was the first time I had made the threat, and they did not like that.

"Surely you won't shoot us!" they said.

I lifted the rifle into the air and fired. That was enough for the trolls. The sound of my rifle sent them running in terror, and that was the last of their tormenting. They were gone, and they would be gone forever. In the end, I realized how easy it was to send them away, considering all they had done.Now I had time to clean the house in peace. My family came home a few hours later. All I had to do was explain to them what had happened to the livestock and broken windows and furniture.

That was the longest week of my life, that three years ago. The trolls never came back. It wasn't until recently when I learned that baby trolls are easily scared. So, if ever you find yourself tormented by them, remember that you are braver than they are. Stand up for yourself, and the baby trolls will leave you be.

Lupendax

Not long ago, in a land not so far away, there was a nasty drought that came upon the face of the land. You may even remember it. Everyone suffered from the scarcity of water and the famine that came soon after. Many creatures tried their best to continue honest lives, but some of them didn't try at all. One such was a wolf, Lupendax, leader of his pack. Since the droughts came, he relied on his craftiness and deception. And it worked for him. It worked so well to deceive other creatures that he took pride in his intelligence. One day, his pack targeted a lonesome buck who was desperately searching for good grass to feed on, so Lupendax went to work. He approached the buck with a piece of paper.

"Hard times are upon us," said Lupendax. "It's too bad some of us cannot find good food."

"Indeed, I agree," replied the buck.

Lupendax smacked his lips. "Well then, I suppose you aren't interested in my offer. Think of this, a land green with healthy grass; perfect for a starving stag like yourself. This is a contract to own such land. No need to read it. All it says is your agreement to own the land that is green with grass. This offer is your only chance and it may never come again. Do we have a deal?"

The buck's eyes lit up. He never imagined owning land of his own with all the grass he could eat!

"Of course, I accept! I agree to you contract!" he said. He pressed a hoof on the contract as his seal of approval.

Lupendax withdrew the paper. "Then it is settled. The land you now own is due south. Congratulations."

Happy as a fawn, the buck bounded away to the deal of his life. But when he reached the land, the grass was brown rather than green. This grass could not be eaten! Then the buck found a sign that read, "Property of His Majesty the King".

"What is this?" cried the buck. "This grass is no good; and it is the King's? That wolf granted me false land!"

The buck, angry with Lupendax, fumed back home. But before he left his supposed land, he heard the howl of many wolves. Then, to his shock, he found himself surrounded by the pack! He tried to run; he tried to fight back, but there were too many wolves. They devoured the buck piece by piece.

The wolves had their fill, and they ate merrily. But a week later, they began to feel hungry again. They soon learned of a family of bears who were very sick and could not fend for themselves. Lupendax took advantage of this. He went to the bears' cave with a new contract. When the husband bear saw him, he grew suspicious. "Why are you here?" he asked.

"Hard times are upon us," said Lupendax. "It's too bad some of us cannot find good water."

"Just get on with your business, wolf," demanded the husband bear.

Lupendax presented the contract. "Here is your chance to own your own river. Clean water, plenty of fish, and dozens of bushes of your favorite berries is not too far north. If you agree with this contract, the river is yours."

"I'm not convinced," said the husband bear. "You seem too anxious."

The wife bear appeared. She was sicker than her husband. "Oh, listen to him, my love. We need the clean water if we're to get better."

"I'm still not convinced he is truthful," said the husband bear.

"But we are sick!" wept the wife bear. "I'm willing to take the chance."

At last the husband bear gave in. "Very well. We agree to your contract." He poked a hole through the contract with his claw as his seal of approval.

"Great!" exclaimed Lupendax. "You won't regret this! Like I said, the river is just due north of here. Congratulations!"

The husband bear was still reluctant, though his wife was excited. But as they traveled north, they found no river.

"What is this?" growled the husband bear. "Where's the water? Where's the fish? Where are the bushes of berries? Didn't the contract-"

"Oh, we have been swindled!" wept the wife bear. "I had such hope!"

Just then, they heard the howl from the pack of wolves. As bears, they should have been able to fight. But since they were sick and weak, they couldn't fight so well. The pack surrounded them and then devoured them, piece by piece.

The wolves had their fill, and they ate merrily. But five weeks later, they began to feel hungry again. This time Lupendax was sure he could swindle the King himself. Now this King did not own a lot, especially during the drought. He was also very poor, and Lupendax knew that. He went to the King's palace with a new contract and scratched at the door.

"Hello," said the King, opening the door.

"Hello, your Majesty. Hard times are upon us," said Lupendax. "It's too bad some of us are not rich, especially you, o' King."

"You have spoken my thoughts," said the King.

Lupendax presented the contract. "Then I suppose you wouldn't be interested in the gold I have. In fact, I have lots of gold; so much that you and your Royal family would need to head east and fetch it yourself."

The King stroked his beard. "Gold can help us during this drought," he said.

His wife the Queen appeared. "May I suggest we read the contract first?"

"Be my guest," said Lupendax.

The Queen took the contract inside to review with her daughter.

"All it says is that the gold is ours," said the Queen. "I see nothing wrong with this. But I am suspicious about the wolf. He seems too anxious."

"What about this fine writing at the bottom, Mother?" questioned the daughter. "See it?"

The Queen reviewed the contract again. "Well bless me, my child! Your little eyes are sharper than mine. What does it say?"

"I don't know. It is too small to read."

That did not stop the daughter. She left for a minute then came back with a magnifying glass.

"Clever!" exclaimed the Queen.

When the daughter gave the Queen the glass, she peered over the fine writing. It said, "In the event that there is no gold, the pack is free to eat the beneficiary."

Frightened at what she had read, she showed it to the King, who read it as well.

"Good heavens! What is this? I knew something was with that wolf!"

Crumbling up the contract, the King opened the door to confront Lupendax.

"There is no gold, is there? You wish to eat us! Well, you will never trick anyone in my kingdom again! As of now, you are banished from my land. Leave now or you will get eaten yourself!"

Upset and humiliated, Lupendax snarled and barked. "You should have accepted the contract! We will eat you anyway!"

He howled to his pack to surround the King. Hearing the howls himself, the King locked himself and his family inside the palace. The wolves tried to break in, but were unable to. They remained at the door until the King's men forced them back with bayonets.

"We've never had to fight enemies such as this before!" complained one of the wolves.

"Lupendax, give us food; not death," said another.

Lupendax didn't care what the pack said. Under his command, the wolves fought back and bit several soldiers. But the soldiers killed many wolves and drove the rest away.

"Let that be a lesson," said the King as the pack retreated. "Never swindle anyone again. If you are to hunt, hunt with dignity and honesty."

"Never mind him," Lupendax told his pack. "Attack and get your fill!"

The pack did not obey Lupendax this time. With several of the wolves dead, and the surviving angry with Lupendax, they decided to leave their foolish leader. Lupendax was left to fend for himself. He was too prideful to run, and so he continued to fight. He fought ferociously, but there were too many bayonets. He fought until they tore him up, piece by piece.

And so was the end of Lupendax. The pack was glad that they were free. When they were far away from the King's land, they promised to hunt honestly. It was harder to get food, but it was the better choice. Not once did they consider swindling other creatures. And therefore, no one was ever offered the Devil's contract in the King's land again.

Michael's Trial

The Curse

MICHAEL WAS ON HIS WAY HOME WHEN THE TROUBLE began. His friend Vincent had gone to visit his uncle for a week and Michael had made the trip with him. Vincent may have been young to be traveling without his parents, but he and Michael were responsible and trustworthy. Michael was with him so Vincent would not have to make the trip alone. At the time, nobody would have ever guessed that the greatest trial in Michael's life, and in the lives of those close to him, was about to come forth.

It had been a long trip for Michael and Vincent, and they were both tired of sitting in a hot car. Since they had the money, they decided to spend a day resting. They found a motel in the next city and agreed to stay there for the night. The two young men checked into their room that was opposite the motel's superb outdoor lounge. As they unloaded their luggage, they saw a man and his wife settling in the room next to theirs.

"One night here and we'll be home by tomorrow," Vincent said to Michael.

"Good. This has been a long trip," Michael replied, stretching and yawning.

They continued unloading their luggage when they happened to cross paths with the married couple. Vincent and Michael stopped. They realized that these people were the Lenwoods. They were famous actors! It was an astounding coincidence that they would be staying in the room next to the Lenwoods!

"It sounds like you two have traveled far," said Mrs. Lenwood to the boys.

"We certainly have," answered Vincent.

"How exciting," said Mr. Lenwood. "We haven't traveled far on this trip. Not as far as you have, at least. But we do travel a lot. We've been in many productions."

Mrs. Lenwood sighed dreamily. "Oh, yes. I remember our first stage performance together. That was before we were married. Time goes by so quickly."

Michael was too shy to say anything other than a simple hello.

"Well, good luck on your journey home," Mr. Lenwood said to him and Vincent.

"And good luck to you, wherever your acting takes you," said Vincent with a friendly wave.

The Lenwoods continued on their way. Michael watched them go. "I never knew we would spend the night next to the Lenwoods," he said.

"Staying here overnight will be interesting indeed," said Vincent.

What would happen later that day would not just be interesting, but rather terrifying. Neither of them knew what was yet to come.

Michael and Vincent did not want to spend the entire day in their motel room. The weather was wonderful, so they decided to tour the small city. There were plenty of things to do, and there were many places to visit. The day went by quickly. After lunch, they found a fairly good-sized park. There were many tall trees and a path that wound through them. Cutting through the park was a rushing river. The sound of the rapids sang throughout the little forest. While exploring the magnificent park, Michael and Vincent were discussing their journey home. Not a soul passed them on the path until a strange woman emerged from the woods. Despite the woman's gray hair, she did not seem that old. She had a long nose, a repulsive smile of yellow-green teeth, and wore a black cloak. She pulled her hood around her head when she saw the two friends.

"Well, what fine people I have met today. I've never seen you two around here before." Her voice was smooth yet fragile.

Neither Michael nor Vincent knew what to say to such a person.

The woman laughed. "You seem worried about my appearance. No need for worry. I'm a witch."

Michael, uncomfortable as he was, tried to be kind by giving a polite nod. Vincent, however, chuckled at the claim. He did not think she was a real witch.

The woman chuckled along with him. "I see why you think it's funny. You have never met a witch before, have you? I believe you have never seen a witch practice her sorcery, then?"

Vincent snorted again in laughter then placed a hand over his mouth in embarrassment. "I'm sorry. I didn't mean to be rude."

Michael finally spoke up, "Can you practice magic if you really are a witch?"

"Why certainly!" said the woman. "Let me show you. Follow me."

Michael and Vincent watched as the self-proclaimed sorceress beckoned them to come off the path. Vincent was a little suspicious about following such a strange lady. He did not believe she was a real witch, but rather loony. Michael started following her, but Vincent pulled him back. "I don't think we should," he whispered.

"I just want to be polite," said Michael.

Vincent leaned close to Michael's ear. "I don't trust her. I think she's crazy."

"No need to worry," said the witch. She again beckoned them. "I'll be brief. Just follow me. I mean no harm."

"We won't be long," said Michael. He started following the witch.

Vincent groaned. He asked the heavens that the visit may be quick, then followed Michael. The witch led them away from the path to a small house on the bank of the river. For being in a park, it was well-hidden. The witch opened the rotted door with a single push and offered to let Michael and Vincent go in first. It was oddly cold inside the house. The two friends gaped around the inside of the tiny place. All they could see was a round table in the shape of a tree trunk and shelves full of herbs and liquids. The witch gestured for them to kneel at the short table in the center of the house. The rushing river was heard outside.

"Please tell me a little about yourselves," said the witch.

Michael swallowed, not knowing what to say.

"Why do you ask us that?" inquired Vincent.

"I need some information if I am to show you my sorcery," she said. "I don't mean personal information. Something in general is what I seek. What do you like? What do you wish to become, for instance?"

Vincent did not see any risk in telling the witch about what he liked. "I enjoy traveling. I just visited my uncle's recently. Someday I wish to cross the ocean and explore new places."

The witch nodded, then turned to Michael. "And you?"

Michael wiped his forehead, hesitating to answer.

"No need to be shy," said the witch in a sour-sweet tone. "Don't you want to see my sorcery?"

"I like observing places near my home," Michael finally said. "We live in a valley that has many meadows and farms. I see many animals, especially in the mountains when I go there. The mountains are beautiful. I particularly like red foxes, but I don't see them much. There is one grove of trees that I like best of all. I notice that it is always clean there; nothing seems to pollute it. I really like that grove."

"Foxes, eh?"

Michael nodded.

"It sounds like a grove to love," said the witch, "and now I will show you what I can do."

Reaching for an empty beaker, she placed it on the table. Then she collected various herbs and a cup of water. With careful doses of each ingredient, she stirred it all together with a wooden spoon. (Michael and Vincent could not help but notice that everything in the house was either made of wood or glass.) When everything was mixed, she poured the newly-created mixture into two cups and placed them in front of the young men. The drinks themselves were dark green.

"Take this and you will witness my sorcery," the witch directed.

Both friends eyed their drinks with doubt. Now Michael was becoming as suspicious as Vincent. But still, his curiosity overcame him. He held the drink up to his lips. He got one little sip before Vincent pulled the drink away.

"Thank you very much, good witch. I think we'll get going now," Vincent said. He stood up and grabbed Michael's arm. Michael stood as well and they both headed for the door.

"One sip is all you need," the witch told Michael. "You said you like foxes?"

"Yes," said Michael.

"Well, before the day ends, you will witness my sorcery. Both of you will." She said this in a light tone, while the words themselves sounded dark.

"Thanks. We'll see you later," said Vincent as he closed the door (he did not really want to see her later). He and Michael immediately ran away from the house, back to the path.

"Such a weird lady," Michael commented.

"Hag is a better word," said Vincent when they found the path.

"What do you think she meant by witnessing her sorcery? She seemed to have liked the fact that I said I like foxes," said Michael.

"I don't know what she meant. I don't think she was a witch at all, but we should leave this park before she follows us."

Michael and Vincent left in an instant. They decided not to explore any more, lest the witch might follow them. Instead, they returned to their motel room. For the rest of the day, they remained in their room. Even though they thought the witch was a lunatic, Vincent was not scared. He did not believe the drinks were potions or anything like that. But Michael was a little concerned. He may have not drunk the entire cup, but he had sipped one drop. He sorely regretted doing so. He was not brave enough to deny the drink as

Vincent had done. The witch's words about witnessing her sorcery before the end of the day repeated itself in his mind. It was a disturbing thought, even though he did not believe it. Michael tried to think about other things. It became much more difficult when he felt a sensation, like an invisible force, crawling up his nose. He decided not to say anything to Vincent, for he believed the strange feelings would pass.

Later that evening, after Michael and Vincent had had their supper, they sat in the motel's outdoor lounge. As they talked and jested with one another, clouds in the dark sky loomed overhead. The moon appeared to be a blurry spot of light amidst the cover. An icy wind started to blow. It was soft yet noticeable, especially for a summer evening. At least there were several lights in the lounge.

"A storm must be coming," said Michael.

"The breeze feels nice," replied Vincent.

Michael took a deep breath. His nose had felt much clearer since that afternoon. He thought he could actually smell better than before. Vincent giggled when he saw Michael sniff the air.

"Maybe the witch's drink has done its effect on you, Michael. I've never seen you sniff like that before."

"It feels great. That drink really changed me," Michael joked.

They both started laughing when Mr. and Mrs. Lenwood came into the lounge. They sat on a couch opposite of Michael and Vincent. Michael stopped laughing and sat down.

"What a chill," said Mr. Lenwood. "Not once have I felt this cold at this time of year."

"I come from a cold place and I would feel this weather all the time," said Mrs. Lenwood. She had a bright smile on her face.

"What did you do today, if you don't mind my asking?" asked Vincent. He wanted this opportunity to converse with the actors.

Mrs. Lenwood sighed a happy sigh. "Oh, nothing private or anything like that. My husband and I are returning to the stage. We want to have a fresh start with our acting. All our big productions can get exhausting after a while. We've decided to take a short break from that. We're really excited."

"You must miss the stage performances then," said Vincent.

"Oh, we do. We saw the theater for the first time today. It's a pleasant, old building, except with all the mice and rats in it. Eah! They're nasty little things. I've never been one to like wild or feral things. It makes me uncomfortable. But I can hold a pet rat as long as it doesn't carry any diseases."

Vincent nodded. "I feel the same way, except I live on a farm. It's something I must deal with."

"As do I, or else I wouldn't return to the stage. Many theaters can be home to mice and rats."

Vincent talked with the Lenwoods for several minutes. He enjoyed the company of such famous people. Michael, however, remained quiet. He did not say a single word to the Lenwoods. Vincent soon noticed that he was no longer in a cheerful mood. His face was pale-white, and his eyes were bloodshot red. His ears and hands had turned a shade darker.

"Michael, do you feel sick?" Vincent asked.

Michael's arms quivered. "I must've eaten something bad," he said.

Vincent was about to ask if it was the witch's drink that was causing the illness, but Michael started wheezing. His chest heaved back and forth. Vincent was very concerned now. "Do you need something?"

Michael did not answer. He held his arms and legs together, his whole body trembling.

"Is there something we can do?" asked Mr. Lenwood.

Michael shook his head, wincing.

"Maybe we should leave," said Mrs. Lenwood.

Vincent thought that that was a good idea. The actors left quietly after saying goodbye to Vincent and wishing good health to Michael.

The clouds now covered the entire sky. The icy wind became stronger; it was no longer soothing. Michael started coughing. He did not stop until he coughed drops of blood. His ears and hands became darker, almost completely black.

Vincent anxiously paced around Michael. "This is serious. Should I take you to the hospital?"

Michael stopped coughing and wiped away the blood from his lips. "I'll be fine." He coughed a few more times. "Stay here. I'll be back."

Michael left for his room and closed the door. Vincent was alone in the lounge. The wind became colder and stronger. For every minute that passed, his heart raced faster.

Michael never came out of the room.

Vincent could not wait any longer. He left the lounge and knocked on the door.

"Michael, can you hear me? What's wrong?"

There was no reply. Vincent placed his ear on the door, hoping to hear his friend. There was a noise, but Vincent did not know what he was hearing. He unlocked the door. When he looked in the room, Michael was nowhere to be found. His clothes were bunched on his bed, and there were a few more stains of blood on the floor. Vincent looked in the space between the wall and one of the beds. The moment he saw Michael, his heart felt like it stopped. His hands trembled. The wind howled outside.

Standing still, his head down, facing the corner, was Michael. His feet and ears were black, his coat was bright, and he had a brush for a tail.

That mad woman *was* a witch!

Vincent let out a cry. Michael had turned into a red fox! One sip of the drink had done just that! Vincent did not know what to do. He panicked, more so than Michael did. Michael was silent, keeping his muzzle in the corner of the wall. Vincent backed a few paces. "Michael! Oh, Michael!"

The Lenwoods appeared at the room's open door after hearing Vincent's cries. They saw his wide eyes from the terror he had just witnessed.

“What’s wrong?” asked Mr. Lenwood.

“Is it your friend?” said his wife.

Vincent returned to his room, keeping the door open for the Lenwoods to walk in.

“The witch! She did this! Michael is a fox! He’s a fox!”

The Lenwoods were confused. Vincent pointed to the corner where Michael stood. When the actors saw him, they froze. No one knew what to do. Michael continued staring at the corner where nobody could see his face. He panted from the traumatic experience.

“Oh, what can we do?” cried Vincent.

Mrs. Lenwood cupped her hands together, as if she knew exactly what had happened to Michael. “I don’t believe it… I don’t. This boy… an animal! A fox! He’s gone rabid, savage… I… is he…”

“I don’t think he’s rabid,” said Mr. Lenwood. “We don’t know what’s going on in his mind right now. He might remember us.”

After Vincent managed his breathing, he made his way to Michael. He stood right at his brush.

“Michael? This is Vincent. Can you look at me?”

Michael did not turn around. The fox was still panting, his tongue hanging out of his mouth. Mrs. Lenwood gasped. “I knew it. A wild animal…”

“Is there anything we can do?” asked Mr. Lenwood.

Vincent sat on his bed. “No. There’s nothing we can do. Oh, poor Michael. Mr. and Mrs. Lenwood, will you please not tell anyone about this?”

“You have our word,” said the actors.

Vincent told them where they lived in case their help was needed. There was nothing else to say after that, so the Lenwoods left. Vincent stayed on the bed, gazing down at Michael. He listened to him panting. Vincent did not say anything. Instead, he said a prayer for Michael in his heart. Michael’s panting soon slowed, and Vincent opened his eyes. For the first time as a fox, Michael turned around and looked up at him. There was something in those dark eyes, something that had always been in Michael's eyes.

"Michael?" said Vincent. "Is that you?"

The fox closed his eyes and bowed his head. It was no nod, but Vincent knew the fox said yes. It was Michael! He was still his friend! Vincent did not take his eyes off him. "The drink actually turned you into a fox," he said. "Can you understand me?"

Michael bowed his head again. Even though Vincent was still shaken and frightened, he felt a little relieved. Michael looked back at Vincent and yawned. It was not a yawn of fatigue, but a yawn of fear. He started trembling as well.

"Don't worry, Michael," said Vincent. "Can you say something? Try to speak."

Michael did not say anything immediately. After another nervous yawn, he tried to say his first word as a fox.

"Elp. Elp… Help."

His voice was completely different. It had such a high pitch. Michael shamefully yawned again.

Vincent understood Michael's shame. "Don't worry, if it's possible for you to become a fox, then it's possible for you to become human again."

With those words, Michael sighed. His breaths now sounded shallower than before. He lay on his belly and placed his black paws over his muzzle. Vincent watched as he started making short, stiff yips. It sounded as if he was crying. This made Vincent shed a few more tears.

The wind continued to howl that whole night. Vincent stayed in his motel room, keeping Michael company. Michael did not make a single vocal sound. All Vincent heard was his shallow breathing. Vincent occasionally spoke to Michael to cheer him up, but he was silent for most of the night as well. He was thinking about the recent events. When the first crack of dawn came through the window, Vincent opened the door to his room. He told Michael to take a breath of fresh air. Michael stepped out of the room. Once he was outside, he sniffed the air as any fox would, then he trotted around the motel grounds. Luckily at that early hour, there was no one else around. Michael had his nose to the ground, looking as if he was tracking something. Vincent became concerned. He did not want Michael to wander off, so he called him back.

Michael stopped tracking whatever scent he found and returned to the door to their room.

"Can you stay here?" asked Vincent. "I don't want you to be in any danger."

Michael bowed his head.

"Good. We planned to go home today. But your mother… I don't know what to say. I don't want to shock her."

Michael was still for a moment, then he spun in a circle. Vincent was baffled, not knowing what Michael was doing. Michael spun again. Of course! He was trying to say something to him!

"Do you have an idea?" Vincent asked.

Michael bowed his head, spun in another circle, and then trotted away. Vincent followed.

"Michael, slow down! Where are you going?"

It was not easy keeping up with Michael. As a fox, he was much faster than before. And he was not even running. Michael turned at the edge of a street, then looked left and right. When he found what he was looking for, he ran up to the city post office, which was not too far from the motel. He stood on two feet, keeping himself balanced by the brick wall.

Vincent caught up to him. "What are you doing here? I don't want you going out into the streets."

Michael started beating his paws on the side of the post office wall, making a strange whine as he did so.

"What are you doing?" asked Vincent.

It was difficult to understand what Michael was trying to say. Michael continued beating the wall while making short whines. He continued doing so until Vincent had an idea as to what he was saying.

"Do you want me to write a letter to your mother?"

That guess was correct. Michael dropped on all fours and bowed his head.

"That's a good idea, except I don't think the letter would reach your mother before we return home."

With a snort, Michael sat down. Vincent tried to think of something else he could do. "My only idea is the telephone," he said.

Michael did not respond.

"I believe the phone is the best choice," Vincent decided.

He returned to the motel room and used the telephone there. A feeling of unease pressed down on Vincent. There was no telling how Michael's mother would react to such news. When he heard Michael's mother on the other end of the line, he gulped. He did not want to give such news to Michael's mother, but he gave a brief explanation about the witch and Michael's curse. With that said, he hung up. He placed his hands over his face, knowing that Michael's mother was also in tears. Vincent left his room, but Michael was nowhere to be found. Vincent became worried. He called for his friend. Michael came from around the corner of the building and his eyes met Vincent's.

"Your mother knows," said Vincent.

Michael tilted his head, as if he did not understand him. This made Vincent feel more nervous. He repeated what he had just said, only slower and more fluent. With that, Michael laid down on his side. He started breathing shallow breaths as he had done before. Vincent knew he understood that time and knew Michael was distressed. Now that his mother was aware of the curse, it was time to go home. But first, Vincent wanted to find the witch. If she was able to turn him into a fox, she could possibly change him back. Vincent packed his and Michael's luggage in the car. Michael jumped in like any pet dog would and laid on the passenger's seat.

"We'll see if we can find this witch," said Vincent.

He drove to the park where they had met the witch the day before, sure to find the tiny house on the bank of the river. He left Michael in the car. The park was big, and Vincent was worried that Michael would disappear and never be seen again. He did not know how Michael would fare to such instincts in a wooded area. It did not take long for Vincent to find the witch's house away from the path, much to his relief. Maybe there *was* a way to get Michael back! Whatever happened, Vincent knew he should avoid any sort of drink or supplement. He did not want to fall at the mercy of a similar curse. Shivering from the howling wind, Vincent knocked on the rickety door. He looked up as he waited. The tall trees blew and waved in the wind.

There was no answer at the door, so Vincent opened it himself. How strange, the table was gone and the shelves were empty! The witch was gone and she had taken everything with her! A new storm of fear loomed in Vincent's heart. There was no hope for Michael if the witch was gone!

Vincent left the house and searched throughout the park. There was no sign of the witch anywhere. Vincent even asked whomever he could find. Nobody had seen her. Full of disappointment, anger, and deep sorrow, Vincent returned to the car. Michael was staring at him through the window. He made more of those strange whining noises when Vincent opened the door.

"I'm sorry for leaving you in here, Michael. I didn't find the witch anywhere. She's gone. I guess now we must get used to this."

Vincent sat in the car as a freezing rainstorm started falling outside. He kept his face buried in his hands. There was no end in sight, no way he could get Michael back. He was right, they had to get used to it.

Vincent felt cold and alone when Michael placed his two forepaws on his lap. Michael was again staring at him with his dark eyes. Vincent placed a hand on Michael's scruff. His coat was thinner than he expected, but it was very soft. A sense of peace slowly settled over Vincent. Michael was not gone. He was still there, the very same person! They were both good friends. Nothing was going to change that.

The feel of Michael's scruff gave a little hope to Vincent. Hope always had to be present if they were to carry on. The rain was falling when they left for home. Rain never affected Vincent's driving a whole lot anyway. The journey home was still long, no less. They traveled all day. Many thoughts ran through Vincent's mind during that time. He wondered what the Lenwoods were feeling at the moment. Mrs. Lenwood was quite frightened when she saw Michael. Then there was Michael's mother. She was weeping when Vincent had last heard her on the phone. Hopefully she would be able to manage such a terrible ordeal.

Many hours later, Vincent arrived at Michael's home. The drive had been very long, but they made it. Vincent opened the passenger door for Michael. When Michael leapt out, he sniffed the moist air (it seemed to have rained here, too). Michael seemed to be doing that a lot. He followed some trail and disappeared behind the car. His mother opened the front door and walked out. She hugged Vincent.

"Thank you for bringing him home," she said. "I was in so much despair when you told me what had happened. I wanted to tell someone, but I didn't think that was a good idea. I didn't know what to do. Carrying on throughout the day made me think. I had time to calm down. Is Michael, you know, *Michael*? Will he remember me?"

"I believe he will. He remembers me," replied Vincent.

When his name was mentioned, Michael returned and stared at his mother. His mother knelt down, weeping again when Michael allowed her to hug him. Their hearts called for each other as they embraced.

"He is soft. He may be a fox, but he is still my son. I love him so dearly. His father does, too. I know he is watching us right now."

Michael's mother continued to hug him when their dog came from inside the house. The dog stopped and sniffed when he saw Michael. Vincent was worried that the dog would attack, but the dog showed no sign of hostility. He instead whined and ran off with his tail between his legs.

"He knows like the rest of us," said Michael's mother.

"And only we know," said Vincent. "As much as we wish to, I don't think we should tell anyone about this."

Michael's mother stood back up after hugging her son. "I agree. We live in a good community. You remember when I told you about the time when Alban Erikson saved Michael's life several years ago? He jumped right in the pond before Michael drowned. He is a good man. We won't tell him or anyone else, but I believe Michael is safe. They won't go after him just because he is an animal, as long as he stays out of trouble."

"I hope so," said Vincent.

That evening, after taking a brief nap in his bedroom, Michael wanted to be outside. Michael's mother believed that he did not want to be confined in such a close space. She allowed Michael to roam outside, but she worried for him. She did not know how Michael's new instincts would affect him, but she did not think he would disappear into the wilderness or anything like that.

Vincent stayed at Michael's home for a while, discussing with Michael's mother of the new trouble in their lives. They continued talking when there was a knock on the door. Michael's mother answered it. Vincent saw that it was Alban Erikson who was the visitor.

"Vincent, I'm glad to see that you're home," the man said. "How was your visit to your uncle's?"

"It was a great visit, Mr. Erikson," said Vincent.

Mr. Erikson looked around. "Now where would Michael be? He's always been such a fine lad. Is he around?"

Michael's mother wiped her eyes to make sure there were no tears. "He's gone right now. I think he wanted fresh air after the long trip."

Mr. Erikson stroked his beard. "I see. Please tell him that I'm glad he and Vincent are home safely. I have to go into town right now before the market closes, so I'll see you later."

Vincent yawned after Mr. Erikson left.

"You seem tired, Vincent. Maybe you should go home. You've

also had a long trip," Michael's mother suggested.

"But what about Michael?" asked Vincent.

"Don't worry about him. I'll watch him and make sure he stays out of trouble. Foxes are known to be mischievous, but I'll make sure Michael isn't."

Vincent did not want to leave Michael, but he knew going home was the better choice. When Michael's belongings were unloaded, Vincent traveled home. He noticed that Michael's mother was taking the whole experience quite well. Michael himself did not seem too distressed after a while. Vincent sorely hoped there was a way to help him.

The Trial

LIFE WAS NOT EASY FOR MICHAEL, BUT ADAPTING TO THE LIFE of a fox was not as bad as he expected. If anything, it was more of a strange experience. Now that he was back home, he was calmer than before. He first noticed, as a fox, that his hearing was far more keen. He was even able to hear the faint sound of a rodent digging in the ground below his feet. And with his nose, he could now smell many new things. But due to his lack of experience, he could not identify every scent he found. Some things he smelled were interesting. Michael liked to follow a particular scent's trail, but he did not want to wander too far from home. Like Vincent, Michael worried that he himself could wander off and never return. However, being aware of this fear eased the dread.

Michael was well aware of the things that had happened to him. He remembered Vincent's panic and Mrs. Lenwood saying he was savage and rabid. Michael could still understand what people were saying, as long as they were not speaking too fast or too slurred. The English language simply sounded like a foreign language he had just learned. On that dreadful night, Michael was afraid that he would lose himself. That was why he had not moved from the corner of the motel room: he was unsure of his fate. But the longer he stayed still, the more his mind cleared from that terrible event. All was not lost. He felt like Michael. He felt like himself! That thought made the enduring of his trial a little bit easier. A little bit. The fact was, he was a fox. Michael debated whether he should try to live like his former self, pretending like he was still a human, or adapt to the life as a wild fox. Michael knew that he was still a human in spirit, and at the same time, the places he knew (his own bedroom for instance) felt more like prisons than a sanctuaries. Perhaps wild foxes did not like being confined in enclosed spaces with few exits. Michael made the decision to live outside to satisfy his instincts, yet he stayed near his home.

When night came and Vincent left for home, Michael did not feel the least bit tired. He did after the abysmal change, but now he had so much energy. He could see very well in the dark, so he decided to look for a temporary place of safety. A den, maybe.

Michael thought he knew of a good place to make a den. Finding a small, grassy mound behind his house, he started to dig. Clawing at the soft dirt was easy. He continued on his task for about ten seconds then stopped. Something did not feel right. Michael looked down at his paws. His claws were caked with mud. This was something Michael was not used to. He always kept his fingernails clean. Getting them this dirty was not comfortable. I just need to ignore it, he thought.

Michael continued digging until he was bored. It was a very tedious chore. He did not even make a good enough tunnel. All he made was lousy depression in the mound. Frustrated, Michael abandoned his new burrow with a snort. Maybe there was something else he could do in the meantime. There were many scents that he could track, so he started following some unknown trail. He continued following it when there was another peculiar scent in the air. It smelled fresh and moist. Michael continued sniffing when a bright flash appeared in the dark sky, followed by a loud bang.

There was another storm brewing.

A few minutes later, the rain began falling. Michael was excited. He used to love rainstorms. He wandered around the yard when another bolt of lightning flashed overhead. The bang of thunder followed it. The rain soon became merciless in the strong wind. No longer did Michael like the storm. He wanted to find shelter immediately. He could not dig a burrow in such furious weather. The only place to go was inside the house.

As Michael trotted to the front of the house, he stopped. He could have sworn he saw something on the mound from the corner of his eye. He looked over his shoulder. What he saw was some sort of glow, not very bright, but noticeable. Curious, Michael had to find out what it was. He was about halfway across the yard when he saw something sniffing at the entrance of his failed den. It was another fox! Michael was initially afraid, thinking this other fox would attack him. But there was something strange about this creature. It was the fox that was emitting the glow. Michael was no longer sure if it was real or a hallucination. Still, Michael was curious. He slowly crept to the mound when the mysterious fox looked up at him. Michael halted, not knowing what to do. The fox sat down and said, "And what can I do for you?"

Michael nearly jumped. It actually spoke to him! He wanted to reply, but he did not want to embarrass himself again. He remained silent.

The fox snorted. "Too ashamed, eh? Don't worry, I understand."

Michael was baffled. Everything about the fox was mysterious. He did not know what to think of him.

"Don't mind me," said the fox, as if he read Michael's mind. "You have a lot to learn, considering what's happened to you. Sad. Very sad. As a boy, you were taught the precious knowledge of good and evil, and you gave in to the powers of evil. Foolish, if you don't mind my saying that. You shouldn't have meddled with things you don't know about. Now look at yourself."

Michael sadly looked down at his black paws being pelted by the cold rain. He felt bad about trusting the witch, all because he was too scared to refuse the drink.

"I hope you've learned your lesson," the mysterious fox continued. "Maybe you can right this wrong."

Michael knew the fox meant well, but he did not like it. He began trembling, his ears were flat and pointed back. The mysterious fox began to laugh at him.

"What's the matter, young one? You seem more confused than I thought. Is it because I also have the appearance of a fox? Well, I'll tell you this, I have always been a fox; unlike you, obviously. What are you afraid of? Your nature? Are you scared that you'll be overtaken, not being able to control yourself?" The fox gave a sly wink.

Michael whimpered, which made the fox laugh even more. The creature stood up from the mound and began walking away. Despite Michael's fear, he had some questions he wanted answered. What if this fox had information on how to break his curse?

"Stop!" Michael barked. For the first time under his curse, he finally said something in the new tongue.

The fox stopped and turned. This time he was serious. "Take care, young one," he said in a calm voice. "If you know not to play with unknown forces, then maybe you will know a good spirit when you see one."

Michael began whimpering again. Was this fox… a ghost? He approached it, but all the fox said was, "Take care, young one." Then he bounded away. In a split second, he was gone. Michael searched frantically for the fox, but there was no trace of him; no sight, smell, or sound. This made Michael even more terrified.

The thunder and lightning came again. The sudden flashes and noises were too much for Michael. His heart raced. First, he was scared because of the thunder, now it was the ghost. This ushered in other bad thoughts that formed a storm of its own inside Michael's mind. The witch, the drink, the change, the ghost, everything. There was no refuge that Michael could find on his own. Life itself frightened him. When the lightning flashed, he saw things off in the distance; unknown things. They looked like terrible monsters coming to prey on him. Michael did not know if he was imagining things or if there really was something out there that was after him. Every time the lightning flashed, whatever was stalking him seemed to be getting closer... and closer.

As scared as Michael was, he approached the strange things when, off in the distance, he heard an unusual noise. It was sort of a chuffing noise.

The lightning flashed again, then came the thunder that rang in his ears.

Michael felt his soaked tail curling around his legs. His own home where he lived his whole life felt alien! Not once had his home seemed so frightening.

The chuffing sounded as if it was getting closer when Michael suddenly heard a scream, a terrible scream! Michael's ears stayed flat. The scream may have come from the distance, but it was worse than the thunder. Michael turned his head to see where the scream came from when a dark figure loomed over him. The monster was tall and hideous. It had many arms that waved about, trying to grab him!

Michael barked in horror and ran. He ran around his house to the front door. He cried and scratched at the door, hoping it would open. Being the middle of the night, Michael did not think that his mother would be awake. Despite that, he scratched on the door, hoping the ugly monster was not looking for him.

Michael was ready to run away when the door opened. His mother looked down at him. Michael bounded into the house and shook the wetness from his coat. A sense of shock zapped him when he felt something touch his back. He looked up to see that it was his mother's hand, which calmed him.

"Michael, is that you?" his mother asked.

The sound of her voice calmed Michael even more. He responded to her question by bowing his head. His mother understood what he was saying by that gesture.

"There's a big storm outside," she said. "You can stay in here. You can any time you want. This is your home, after all."

Michael was glad that his mother was not too troubled. He did not want his awful situation to ruin the lives of the people close to him. His mother returned to her room, leaving Michael alone in the lounge. This time Michael did not feel enclosed. He heard the raging storm outside. At least whatever was out there, the scream or the monster with many arms, could not get him now. Michael's house now felt like the home he knew.

The storm passed by morning. Michael did not think he would sleep, but he did. The cozy feeling of home allowed him to rest. His mother let him go outside when she woke, and Michael was grateful for that. With the sun giving life to the valley, the land no longer seemed scary. It looked like the land Michael knew, though things were not exactly the same. Due to his small size, his eyes were closer to the ground. And his vision was familiar but different. He did not see as many bright colors anymore, but his vision seemed sharper. Anything that moved, no matter how small or slight, Michael could notice.

In the clear weather, the yard was calm compared to the recent night. Michael went around to the back yard. There, he beheld the monster with many arms. It was no monster! It was the willow! Michael felt silly at how he was easily fooled. But if he was fooled by the willow, did something else fool him into thinking that he saw the mysterious fox? Michael examined at the mound. There was nothing there that explained the visit. He was about to sit down in thought when he saw someone that he knew: his dog, Alexander. Michael did not move. Since he had come home, his dog avoided him. Alexander knew it was Michael. How he knew, Michael did not know. Michael tried to make a friendly gesture. But the moment he moved, Alexander ran off. Michael was not worried about him. Alexander was only shocked like everyone else.

Michael sat next to the willow. *What can I do today?* he asked himself. It was not long before he decided to explore nearby places. The storm was gone, and he was no longer scared of wandering off and never returning. The desire to explore felt wonderful. Michael passed several houses that belonged to people he knew. He avoided the houses, even though he did not think he was in any sort of danger. He avoided most especially the homes that had dogs. He did not think the other dogs would behave as Alexander did.

During his little adventure, Michael heard the scream in the distance. It was the same scream from the previous night. Each passing moment it sounded again. It was getting louder. Michael ran, not knowing what was making the horrible noise. He ran through the soft grass when he came across two lines of iron. Rails! They were rails to the railway line that ran through the valley! The scream was the whistle of a train. That was what he had heard last night! Michael was never scared of trains. He knew he was in no danger as long as he stayed off the tracks. After the train passed, Michael continued to explore the land around him. He explored many different groves and fields in the valley until he realized that he was near Mr. Erikson's barn. Michael grew excited. He had great respect for Mr. Erikson; ever since he had saved him from drowning in the pond. He did not expect Mr. Erikson to recognize him, of course. Michael just wanted to see if he could find him. He approached the barn with no sense of caution when he heard someone call his name.

"Michael! Michael!"

No. He did not hear his name. He heard a dog's bark. Michael again approached the barn.

"Michael! Michael!"

Michael tilted his head. Was he hearing things? He could have sworn he heard his name.

"Michael! Michael! I come! Wait!"

He then knew what was happening. It was the bark of a dog who was calling his name! It was a bark that Michael had heard before. Alexander, his own pet, caught up with him. Michael wanted to express his joy, but did not know how. He was happy to see that Alexander was no longer scared of him. He wanted his dog to join him on his adventure. Michael continued on his way to Mr. Erikson's barn. "Follow me," he said in the new tongue.

He looked back at Alexander to see if his dog understood that.

Alexander tilted his head, as Michael had done earlier. The dog was concerned. "To home of bearded man?" he asked.

Michael repositioned his ears. It was not easy understanding Alexander completely. He spoke differently, as if he had an accent. Maybe if they were both dogs, they would understand each other better. A wild fox could only interpret so much of what a domestic dog was saying.

Michael gave an easy, simple answer, "Yes."

Alexander did not approve. "I rather not. I no like home of bearded man, hear? Barn smells nice, for sure, when wind blows right, but man is mean as cat to mouse. You as wild dog, bearded man will get gun. You my friend as man, and I no want to see you dead, hear?"

Michael wanted to say something else, but he was unable to express such words. Alexander left, so Michael continued his journey to the barn alone. When he reached it, the smells of the farm excited him even more. He used to hate the rich odor of Mr. Alban's barn, thanks to three goats, three pigs, a mule, and a cow. Now the barn had a fresh smell to it. The straw! The manure! Michael was unsure if he should be delighted or disgusted. He circled around the barn where he found a flock of chickens: seven hens and one rooster. Also foraging nearby was a flock of tame geese.

Michael stopped dead in his tracks, his full attention on the chickens.

The old fears returned. An urge to take one of the chickens came over him. Mr. Erikson would be upset if he did so. Michael closed his eyes, ready to fight off the unbearable desire. He feared that he would be unable to help himself. The instinctive urge came, sure enough. The clucking of the chickens sounded appetizing (in a funny sort of a way).

Michael opened his eyes. The chickens were disturbed by his presence, but Michael did not move. The instinct was there, but it was not overbearing. Michael knew that attacking the chickens was a bad idea. He turned around, thinking about going to the pond instead. The hens behind him squawked and ran about when he began trotting away. Michael ignored them.

What happened next took him by surprise. He heard the faint footsteps of something running up behind him, then he felt a searing pain on his back. Gray feathers beat violently above his head and angry honks engulfed him. It was one of the geese! Michael yelped in shock as the other members of the flock attacked as well, all honking up a storm. The hens began cackling at all the commotion, which alerted the rooster, which alerted the other animals. Soon the whole farm was up in a noisy frenzy. Michael immediately spun around and snapped his jaws down on the wretched bird's neck. With a single snap, his teeth squeezed the life out of the goose. He dropped the carcass on the ground and spat out the feathers before dashing away until the other geese stopped pursuing him. He was ready to run off back into the woods when he heard the door to Mr. Erikson's house slam shut. Michael looked up to find Erikson running out to the barn. Michael felt guilty. He had not meant to kill the goose. He approached the barn door, hoping to let Erikson know that it was an accident. Maybe he won't be mad if I don't run, he thought.

Mr. Erikson, angrier than Michael thought, came storming back out of the barn. Michael felt the fur on his scruff prickle. Erikson was loading a gun!

Michael ran off the moment he saw it. With the true speed of a fox, Michael reached safety just in time. The ping of a bullet struck just below his tail right when the blast of the gunshot was heard. Hearing the gunshot was far worse than the thunder or the scream of the train the night before. Michael was not imagining anything. This was a real danger! If he could not reach safety in time, he could be killed! Living as a fox was a bad enough experience in Michael's life. Dying as one would be worse, especially when it was by the hand of the man who had once saved his life. Mr. Erikson did not know it was Michael after all. If only he-

Bang! Another gunshot echoed from behind, followed by a second ping right above his head. There was no time to ponder the situation. He had to escape, fast! The reflexes of a fox gave Michael a true advantage. Not only was he able to run quickly, but he could also stop suddenly and dart in another direction. Michael ran this way and that, believing that his best chance of escape came if he did not stop no matter what.

As he fled, Michael came across the entrance to some hole. It was too small for him to slip inside. It was possibly an old rabbit hole. There was no fresh scent inside it. Michael inspected the hole until he heard Mr. Erikson's voice coming from the other side of the meadow. Michael was off again.

Did I really do something bad enough that I should be punished by death? Michael thought. He had never perceived Mr. Erikson like this before. Erikson had always enjoyed hunting, but Michael never thought of him as aggressive. Michael was acting in defense after all! He did not seek to kill any of Erikson's animals. If he did, then Erikson had a good reason for protecting his property; there was justification in that. But now that Michael was the one being hunted, he saw Erikson more as a predator than the warm-hearted man he used to be. No matter, Michael's life was in danger and he had to run. He started running in a straight line when something did not feel right. There was an odd feeling that told him to stop. Michael ignored it and kept running, but the feeling only became stronger. He was gaining distance when he suddenly heard footsteps next to him. These footsteps sounded like his own. Michael looked off to his right and saw the mysterious fox running beside him.

"Use your wits, young one! It was a man who sent me to the next life," the fox said.

Michael stopped. When he looked to his right again, the ghostly creature was gone. There was no trace of him anywhere. Michael heeded his advice, nonetheless. Instead of running in a straight line, he resumed is form of darting in various directions until he crossed the tracks. His wits. Michael had to use his wits if he was to escape. When he reached the edge of his yard, he barked. It sounded different from a dog's bark, but Michael wanted to alert Alexander of the danger.

"Is bearded man after you with gun?" Alexander asked him. "I smell something bad."

"Yes!" cried Michael. "He is coming!"

Alexander followed him to the house. "Bearded man not after me. I go with you anyway. I smell him. He angry."

Michael reached the back door and pawed on it. He waited anxiously for his mother to answer. The second the door was open, Michael raced in and ran straight to his bedroom. Jumping on his bed, he went to lay on his pillow, panting sharply. My pillow, my bed, my room, he thought.

He started to cry after his panting slowed. His short breaths and quiet yips were his way of shedding tears. His mother came in and noticed his distress. "Michael, is there something wrong?" she asked.

Michael did not answer. His mother sat down on his bed and hugged him. She began crying as well, knowing that Michael had a deep internal pain.

"Don't worry, Michael. Therell beeaway t'bringyeback. Beforealong, yee'll be the Michael weall know. Jusstay schrong."

Michael's mind felt like it was spinning. He knew his mother was trying to comfort him. The problem was that she was speaking too fast. Her words sounded jumbled and even a little confusing. He nestled his muzzle in the pillow. Tears formed in his eyes and ran down his face. With his mother already present, he wished Vincent was with him. He, along with his mother, seemed to understand him the best.

As Michael gathered all his thoughts together, he concluded that it was not living as a fox he disliked worst of all. The worst thing was the rash change in his life. He felt isolated, cut off. He may have been able to talk to Alexander (that was something he did like), but he could not say anything that his mother or his friend would recognize. And there was the fact that Mr. Erikson had tried to kill him. Michael kept telling himself that Erikson was only protecting his flock. It was just the fact that… Mr. Erikson had tried to kill him! Fox or man, it was no different. He was nearly killed today!

Michael longed for help. He did not want to be a fox. He did not want people he knew, people he thought he knew, to try to kill him without a single drop of empathy. If he was born and bred into the life of a fox, then a close dance with death would have been a different experience. But he had a different life. He wanted it back! He wanted this nightmare to end!

The Quarry

Mrs. Lenwood dreamt that she was lost in the woods. There was no path to follow, no place to recognize. A black mist flowed through the woods, blocking most of the moonlight. All she could hear was the howl of the freezing wind, the same wind that came on the night the young man had become a fox.

Hearing Vincent's cry for help and seeing the helpless young man haunted her mind like the ghost of a dark memory. Mrs. Lenwood looked all around the woods. She could barely see because of all the mist.

Then came the cry.

It was the cry of a man; a cry of fear. Mrs. Lenwood approached the source of the sound. Maybe she could rescue the young man before it was too late! She would have run had it not been for the gloomy atmosphere.

She eventually arrived at the spot where she thought the scream had come from. In the dark, she saw the figure of some small creature. Though it was hard to see, the animal's coat was bright, except for its ears. The animal had a thick brush that ended with a white tip. It was the fox, facing a tree as it had done in the corner of the motel room. Mrs. Lenwood only saw its back end. She had not yet seen its face.

Mrs. Lenwood spoke, hoping the fox would respond. "Hello?"

The fox did not turn its head, but its ears followed her voice. The fox did hear her.

Again, Mrs. Lenwood said, "Hello?"

She took one step closer, then the fox turned. She saw its face for the first time. Its eyes were dark red, its snarling mouth was covered with yellow foam, the fur on its face was gritty and stained with blood, and its scruff stood straight up. Mrs. Lenwood now wished she had never seen its face.

This was not the young man! It was not him at all! The angry fox growled an angry growl and bounded after her. Mrs. Lenwood ran as fast as she could, but the fox was much faster. She felt its teeth sink into her heel. With a cry, Mrs. Lenwood fell. She turned on her back and saw the fox glaring at her. It was true. It was all true. He *was* a rabid monster!

"Don't hurt me!" she cried.

The fox suddenly vanished. She was again in her bed; sweat soaked her pillow.

Her husband woke as well. "Did you have that dream again?" he asked.

Mrs. Lenwood wiped her forehead. "Yes."

Mr. Lenwood sighed. "We've both been having these dreams for too long. It's been a month since we saw what happened."

"And these dreams keep coming back again and again. What can we do about it?"

Mr. Lenwood was deep in thought for a moment, then he got out of bed. "Gather some clothes. I have an idea."

"And what is that?" inquired Mrs. Lenwood.

"The young man's friend, Vincent, if I remember his name, told us where he lived. I believe the young man will be there, as a fox."

"You want to *see* him as an animal? Wasn't that the cause of these dreams to begin with?"

"It was," said Mr. Lenwood. "We can find him and see what really happened to him. We will see if he really is the monster in our dreams."

Mrs. Lenwood was not sure. "But what if he is? That night, we only saw him from behind. We never saw his face. What if he's a lot worse than in our dreams?"

"Then we will see. Our production had its final curtain. We have time to do this. It will be our only chance to put our fears to rest, even with the risk it brings."

Mrs. Lenwood soon decided that that was the best choice. They left that very night. While in the car, Mrs. Lenwood stared out the window. She did not know what was to come her way with this journey. Just the simple fact that a young man had become a wild creature made her heart race. The journey to the valley was a long one. Neither she nor Mr. Lenwood knew the troubles Michael was facing.

They reached the valley at one o'clock the following afternoon. The countryside was sparsely populated. The Lenwoods thought that a rural community would make it easier to find Vincent, who was their key to finding Michael. They were a bit skeptical about going to random houses and asking for directions, but they did after all. There was no other way they could find Vincent. They came to a farm house and knocked on the door. An old, bearded man answered the door. It was Mr. Erikson.

"Good day. Is there something I can do for you?" Erikson asked. He did not recognize the actors.

"Yes," said Mr. Lenwood. "Can you tell us where a boy named Vincent lives?"

"Why sure. He lives three houses down the road. Are you family?"

"No, but we have met him before. Does he have any close friends nearby?"

Mr. Erikson pointed in the direction where the Lenwoods had come. "He is friends with a boy named Michael. If you came from the west, you already passed his house. I haven't seen Michael in a while. He's such a good young man, always kind and generous. I have great respect for him and Vincent."

"Michael," Mrs. Lenwood repeated. "Thank you, sir. Also, before we leave, has anything unusual been happening around here lately?"

"Well, somebody crashed his car in town yesterday. Luckily he wasn't hurt."

Mrs. Lenwood tried to be as casual as possible. "I see. What about weather? Earthquakes? Strange animals?"

"Hmm. Everything seems to be the way it should. Except there's a dumb little fox running about. He got one of my geese a while ago. He won't get away with it, mark my words. Foxes usually come and go, especially if we kill them. They're no different from skunks, raccoons, or badgers and whatnot. But this one fox is hanging around like he has no home. People occasionally see him. Most want him gone."

Mrs. Lenwood tried to mask her fear from Mr. Erikson. "What will you do if you find him?"

"Kill him, of course," said Erikson, chuckling. "My friends and I have agreed that whoever gets him will have the pelt as a trophy."

Mrs. Lenwood let out a gasp. Erikson frowned. "Sorry. I didn't mean to upset you."

"That's all right," said Mr. Lenwood. "Where did you last see the fox?"

"In the meadows, not too far from Vincent's house. Some of my friends are after it right now. I better join them soon if I'm to win this game of ours."

Both Mr. and Mrs. Lenwood were afraid. They thanked Mr. Erikson (though they were greatly alarmed) and returned to their car.

"Michael. Yes, I remember now. The boy's name is Michael. He's the fox," said Mr. Lenwood.

Mrs. Lenwood felt as if her lungs were cracked ice. "They're after him! Whether he's rabid or not, he's in danger! That man doesn't know it's Michael. He's being hunted even as we speak!"

Mr. Lenwood felt the same way as his wife. "We better find him before they do. We need to find Vincent right now if we're to find Michael. I don't think Michael will be at his house if he's a fox."

He started the car and sped down the road to the third house east. When Mr. Lenwood stopped, his wife jumped out and approached the front door. There was no car or truck present and blinds covered all the windows. It seemed as if no one was at home. Mrs. Lenwood rapped on the door. No answer. She was on her way back to the car when the report of a gunshot echoed across the valley. Mrs. Lenwood's heart raced even faster. She got into the car. "Vincent isn't here. We need to find Michael ourselves."

Mr. Lenwood resumed driving. "I'll follow the gunshot."

Following a sound that echoed throughout the valley was not easy. The Lenwoods guessed that it had come from the north-east. It was obvious they could not go straight in that direction. The roads, most of them dirt roads, formed large grids. The Lenwoods passed through hollows, orchards, and fields, either turning left or going straight through intersections. Not a single car passed them as they traveled. Mr. Lenwood turned left at the intersection just before they reached the level crossing. He stopped there and got out.

"Do you see anything?" asked Mrs. Lenwood, also exiting the car.

"No," replied Mr. Lenwood sadly.

They both listened carefully. There was no second gunshot. They continued listening when the faint sound of a whistle came from the far north. The Lenwoods stayed silent. In between the whistles of the train, they began hearing the baying of dogs coming from the east. Mrs. Lenwood looked in that direction. She saw a group of men in the distance. The dogs were with them. "Do you see that?" she asked her husband.

MICHAEL WAS HUNGRY. OVER THE PAST MONTH, HE HAD grown accustomed to eating mice and occasionally rabbits. He avoided chickens and other small farm animals of the sort, but Mr. Erikson and the men were still after him, often accompanied by hounds or terriers. Michael had grown accustomed to that as well, even though he felt he still lacked the true fox experience to outwit them properly. He wandered through the meadow in search of something to eat when the gunshot came. It was in the distance, so Michael was not too concerned. He continued searching for a quick snack. The meadow was a good place to find food, as long as he was alert for danger. After searching for clues as to where a meal may be, Michael heard a faint digging under a bush. It sounded like a mouse. He lowered himself for the pounce. The waiting game did not bother Michael at all. He did not see the mouse, but he knew exactly where it was. Now for the quick jump…

He leapt right when the sound of a baying dog, a terrier, came from close by. Michael froze, letting the frightened mouse scurry away.

Michael did not recognize the baying. The only dog's voice he truly recognized was Alexander's. The dog that gave tongue was definitely not Alexander. This one sounded hostile! Terrier, hound, or heeler, it did not matter to Michael. What mattered was that this dog was more than likely after him. Forgetting his hunger, Michael began running for his life once again. For the first time in weeks, he feared for his life. And it was not just his death that worried him. He worried about his mother and Vincent: the people close to him who knew he was a fox. He did not like the idea of them discovering his body if he was killed by a man who did not even know who he had just killed.

The baying was heard again; this time it was much closer. Michael left the meadow once he had an idea as to where the terrier may be. He sprinted out of the protection of the trees when he suddenly found himself in front of a man and his weapon! In utter terror, Michael acted on instinct and reflex. He jumped forward and savagely attacked the man's ankle. While the man bent over, cursing at his wound, Michael raced off in the other direction. He ran with his heart beating hard in his chest. He was back in the meadow when he stopped again. His thickening coat stood straight up. Coming towards him was not one but several terriers! There was no time to get a good look at each one. Michael was off in sheer panic. The terriers were fast. Too fast! If I reach the den, then I may still have a chance! he thought.

The terriers were catching up to him, all of them barking as they ran. Michael understood very little of what they were saying.

"Fox! Master come for you, ha! You run fast. I run faster! Ha! Ha! Ha!" The rest Michael could not interpret.

He was close to the old rabbit burrow. Over the weeks, Michael had enlarged it for his own comfort. The burrow had many entrances and exits, making it perfect for refuge in Michael's opinion.

So close! So close and I'll make it. Oh, but the dogs!

Michael reached the hole just in time. With a little squirming, he was able to crawl inside. The terriers were too big to fit, so Michael crawled deeper underground.

"Fox! Dig!" the dogs barked.

There was little time to rest. The other terriers started digging at different entrances. Michael did not feel safe at all. He had to find an open exit, and quick. There had to be one he could use. He made his way through the dark tunnels, even though they were not dark for Michael. He continued making his way until he saw daylight. He climbed out to find that he was not too far from one of the terriers. With its nose buried in the hole, it did not notice him right away. With this head-start, Michael was off. It was not long before the terrier spotted him and was after him. There was no place for Michael to hide. He had to run and hope for the best.

"Oh, help! Somebody, help!"

The sound was a high-pitched cry, but Michael's message was clear. He did not think he would stay ahead for long, but what else could he do? The thought of his mother mourning over his shredded body was a terrible vision.

Soon after the chase began, Michael started to become fatigued. The terrier was getting closer.

"Find strength, young one. Life isn't so easy, is it?"

Michael looked around as he ran. The mysterious fox was not running with him, but Michael heard his voice in the air. Then, off in the distance, came a sound that had scared Michael during his first night home after he was cursed. Now it sounded like the key to escape. The sound of an approaching freight train gave Michael a small burst of energy. He was approaching the main line. If he crossed before the train passed, he may escape the terrier! It was a very risky, but necessary idea. Despite how exhausted he was, Michael kept running. The main line was in sight, and so was the train. This was Michael's only chance. Everything seemed to happen at once. Michael wanted to close his eyes, but he had to keep them open.

The train looked like a large black monster with a white river of steam coming from its slender funnel. It sounded its whistle as it approached the level crossing. The engine itself was too loud for Michael's ears. He jumped over the first rail. The wooden ties shook. He jumped over the second rail. A rushing, moist wind blew past his tail. Before he knew it, Michael found himself running straight into the paths of two people. There was no time to stop and see who they were. Michael ran between the legs of one of the strangers and dove into the brush on the other side of the road. Since Michael made it across the tracks, he could run no more. The terrier was no longer after him. He lay in the thick brush, panting. His lungs burned painfully. The sound of the freight cars and brake van clattered by. Michael stayed in his cover, trying to slow his breathing while keeping his body cool after the enduring run.

The two people standing at the edge of the road were the Lenwoods. Michael did not see them clearly from under the brush. All he saw was Mr. Lenwood cradling his shaking arms and Mrs. Lenwood placing her hands over her mouth.

"There he is! The train just missed him!" exclaimed Mr. Lenwood.

Mrs. Lenwood bent forward. "Michael, is that you?"

Michael did not answer. Not only was he out of breath, but he did not recognize them yet. He found it strange how they called him by his name. Who else knew he was Michael besides Vincent and his mother? The answer suddenly came to him: the Lenwoods!

"Michael, it's us," said Mr. Lenwood. "We are the actors you met at the motel. Do you remember us?"

Michael never expected the actors to be there in the valley. It was a good feeling to see them. The painful thoughts of his death were replaced with good thoughts. The Lenwoods were good people.

Michael did not respond to them at first. Mrs. Lenwood shuttered. "Oh no. It's true. He doesn't remember us. He's truly a feral thing!"

Mr. Lenwood was more determined. "Michael? You remember us, right? Michael?"

Michael felt silly. He was so happy to see them that he did not know how to respond. He stepped out of the brush, still panting. He stared at Mr. Lenwood, then at Mrs. Lenwood.

"Do you remember us?" asked Mrs. Lenwood in a hopeful voice.

For his response, Michael bowed his head. Mr. Lenwood sighed in confusion before realizing what that meant. "He *does* remember us!"

"Oh, Michael, we were so worried." Mrs. Lenwood bent down and stroked Michael's scruff. Over time, his coat had become lush and very soft. Even as a fox it felt awkward, but Michael did not care. He allowed them to touch him.

The sound of a truck soon broke the peace. Michael knew it was Vincent. His friend must have known about the hunt. When Vincent climbed out of the truck, he looked down at Michael, then at the actors. "Mr. and Mrs. Lenwood, I didn't expect to see you here."

"We've been concerned, having not seen Michael since that dreadful night," said Mrs. Lenwood. "Did you see what just happened?"

"I did," said Vincent. "I heard the dogs and became worried. These hunts have been hard on us both, having people you know try to kill your friend just for the sake of sport; nothing else." He gulped. "I used to think they were good people."

Michael watched Vincent brush away a few threatening tears. Vincent talked with the actors, but Michael did not listen. He was still shaken from the close encounter with the terrier and most especially the train. He was paranoid. The dog was nowhere in sight, and Michael did not want it to take him by surprise. Taking a step over the tracks, he looked out over the meadow. The sound of shouting people reached Michael's ears, followed by more baying dogs.

They were coming for him!

Running as he had must have left a good scent for the dogs. Michael interrupted the nearby conversation, whining in fear.

"What's wrong, Michael?" asked Mr. Lenwood.

Michael stared at Vincent and then out to the meadow. Vincent was good at interpreting what Michael was trying to say. Michael was too embarrassed to try any verbal noises in the presence of the Lenwoods.

"I don't hear anything, but Michael knows there is danger coming," Vincent told the actors.

Michael heard the baying of dogs again. The challenge of outwitting dogs felt impossible to overcome while so exhausted. He whined at Vincent; his personal pride was pointless at this moment.

"He's scared," said Mrs. Lenwood.

"I know why," replied Vincent. He bent down to Michael. "Do you know what to do?"

Michael yawned. That was his way of saying no.

"Can you take him back to his house for safety?" asked Mr. Lenwood.

The sound of shouting men was getting closer. Michael did not feel safe, even in the presence of his friends.

"It won't be safe, the people know that he is often around his house," Vincent explained. He then addressed Michael, speaking slowly and fluently, "Michael, go to the abandoned quarry. The Lenwoods and I will be there as soon as we can. It will be a safe place for now. Do you remember the quarry?"

Michael did remember. It was up in the foothills. He and Vincent used to visit it often. The quarry brought promise to the valley once upon a time, but it had been closed for years, since the depression. The idea sounded like a good one, except going there sounded difficult (especially with the thought of dogs nipping at his tail). But what safer place was there to go? His house? The meadow? Vincent could not take him in the truck because the road to the quarry had been washed out last spring. The only way to get there was on foot. With the quarry in mind, Michael ran off, leaving his friends far behind.

The foothills themselves were about a mile and a half away, and Michael took many different paths on his way up there. He ran along wooden fences, through shallow ditches, and sometimes he back-tracked. That may confuse the dogs, he thought.

When Michael finally reached the foothills, he was covered with mud. He started to doubt that he would even reach the quarry alive. His legs were sore, his paws battered, and his chest hurt immensely. He felt like whimpering, but that made the pain even worse. Michael still had a long way to go. As he was on his way up the first slope, a sharp pain seared his right forepaw. He looked down and saw that he stepped on a sharp rock. Blood dripped from the pad of his foot. The pain made Michael's legs tremble, but he had to go on despite the suffering.

What was left of the quarry were a few standing sheds, some rotting equipment, and an unused railway line that branched off from the main line in the valley. Finding the quarry was not hard with the landmarks present. When Michael reached the abandoned site, he collapsed. Every muscle in his legs ached. Breathing was agony. Living was suffering. Michael longed for the pain to cease. Since he was no longer running, some thoughts came into his mind. All this pain because of a goose and a confused farmer! Michael had not ventured near Mr. Erikson's home since that incident, and still he was after him. Erikson was not hunting for food, as with Michael and the mouse; Erikson was not hunting in self-defense, as with Michael and the goose; and Erikson was not hunting to protect his property, hence the first shooting. So why the hunt now? Is it revenge? Is it pleasure? Michael had never known what some animals went through until then. He was in pain, real pain. A man harming his kin is seen as wrong, which it truly is (one of the worse things a man can do). But why was it not wrong to cause pain and suffering to other living things? Being hunted to the point of exhaustion was torture for Michael. How could Erikson, a peaceful and kind man, not be able to see the suffering he was inflicting? Michael did not hate Mr. Erikson, but he wished Erikson would realize what he was doing.

Vincent and the Lenwoods were not at the quarry yet. There was no sight nor sound of his pursuers either, so Michael lay quietly. His chest rose and fell with each wheezing pant. Eventually, the pain in his chest went away. Michael stood back up. His legs were not trembling anymore, but his feet felt very tender. At least he was able to walk. With no sense of danger, Michael laid back down and closed his eyes. Sleep embraced him with welcoming arms. He dreamt of his human life. He remembered his trip with Vincent. It had been fun and exciting. That was until that hag, that *witch*, cursed him to live his miserable life as a fox. What the witch had done was a work of sorcery, dark magic. The forces of evil had invaded Michael's body and changed him. Michael sorely regretted taking that drink. But he had, and now he was living the cruel consequence. The mysterious fox told him about that. In his dreams, Michael wept. His emotions made his heart heavy and weak.

"Is there some way to break this curse?" he asked aloud.

Nobody answered him. Michael continued crying. There had to be a way to break the curse! He felt lost and alone when someone spoke to him. "You're doing well, young one. It took courage to do what you did."

Michael saw the mysterious fox standing in front of him. "Is there some way to break this curse?" he asked again.

"I know there is a way," answered the mysterious fox. "You should not give up hope. Without hope, you won't find an end to your trial."

Michael listened closely. "What is this way? What do I need to do?"

The mysterious fox did not answer. The sound of footsteps came from the slope below. They sounded like human footsteps. The mysterious fox looked over his shoulder then ran off. Michael, now awake, looked to see where the fox had bounded off to, but he was nowhere to be found. Michael got to his feet, wondering who was coming. There was only one set of footsteps. He did not know who it was by scent. There were no baying dogs. Curious, Michael approached the source of the sound. He froze when he saw who it was. Mr. Erikson!

"So, this is where you're hiding, you little devil!" Erikson snapped.

He did not expect to find Michael out in the open; his gun was not ready. As he loaded it, Michael took the precious opportunity and ran. He ran around an old shed for cover. Erikson chased after him. Michael found that behind the shed was another steep slope, going up, and covered with loose rocks. If he made his way up the slope, Erikson would never catch him! Michael immediately began the climb. It brought back the agony from the previous chase. So many sharp rocks kept piercing Michael's paws. The pain in his feet returned and was worse than ever. Michael could not hold back cries and yelps. From the bottom of the slope, Erikson fired his gun. The bullet shattered the rocks off to Michael's left. Every step he took felt like flaming-hot knives stabbing his feet. He continued yelping when Erikson fired again. This bullet whizzed above Michael's back. It struck some rocks that rolled down the slope. Michael scrambled out of the way just in time.

More rocks began tumbling down, many more than Michael had expected. Those at the top lost their secure ground and rolled down as well. It looked like the beginning of a terrible disaster. When Michael looked up again, he saw a large boulder coming down the slope. His lungs felt like they were made of stone. Mr. Erikson was no longer a threat, the boulders were! Michael struggled down the slope as fast as possible. He slipped and rolled over rock after rock until he was at the bottom. Finding whatever strength he had left, he limped to the side just seconds before the boulder came crashing down. It destroyed a shed with a single pass. More boulders came down. Erikson fled, leaving Michael alone. The boulders rolled past him. The small rocks rolled over him. The ground shook as the rockslide gathered strength. The overwhelming pain and noise were too much for Michael. He passed out, half-buried in rocks and stones.

The rockslide only lasted a few minutes, but the damage was done. All that was left of the old machinery were clumps of metal. Several sheds in the quarry were ruined, most were destroyed.

The place was completely quiet when Vincent and the Lenwoods arrived. They did not think any of the hunters would follow Michael to the quarry, not knowing Erikson had been there.

The sound of the rockslide had echoed throughout the valley like thunder. When Vincent and the Lenwoods heard it, they hurried all the faster on the battered trail. The dust had yet to settle when they reached the quarry. All three of them gasped in horror. After the awful noise, there was a ghostly silence. The place felt like a dusty graveyard.

"Where's Michael?" Mrs. Lenwood asked tensely.

Vincent did not answer. He climbed on the fallen rocks and boulders, fearing for Michael's life. He called out Michael's name; there was no response. "Help me look for him!" he cried.

All three searched for Michael. Vincent looked all around but found no trace of a fox. Several minutes passed. The sound of Mr. Lenwood's voice nearly made him lose his balance.

"I found him!"

Vincent made his way to Mr. Lenwood. There was Michael, lying still and covered in rocks. His fur was tattered and caked with blood and filth. There was a deep gash in his hind leg. His lips were slightly unfurled, partially exposing his teeth.

Mrs. Lenwood examined Michael. "He's still breathing," she said.

Hearing that was the best news Vincent had ever received. Michael's legs slowly began moving again. He was severely wounded, but alive. Stirring for a moment, Michael opened his eyes. He stared at Vincent.

"Thank goodness!" Vincent sighed.

Michael tried to stand, the rocks rolling off his body. His right leg could not take his weight. It did not feel broken to him, thankfully, but the gash tortured him awfully.

"We should take him back to his house since no one is after him anymore," suggested Mrs. Lenwood.

Very carefully, Vincent lifted Michael from the cemetery of rocks and stones. Being held in Vincent's arms comforted Michael. He thought he was going to die before he was found. Now it was over.

Michael had not been inside his house for days. His mother was frightened when she saw his wounds, but was relieved that he was alive. "I heard the rockslide while I was caring for my garden," she said. "I did not know Michael was up there."

"Somebody fired a gun when it happened," said Mrs. Lenwood. "I heard it right before the rockslide."

Vincent told Michael's mother of the recent events, how Mr. Erikson was after Michael again and now Erikson and his friends had dogs.

Upon hearing this, Michal's mother stamped her foot. Michael had never seen her so upset, bundled in sadness and anger.

"This can't go on," said his mother. "Michael is staying here in this house. I can't have him roaming the countryside if his life is in danger. I will have a talk with good old Alban Erikson. He nearly killed my son! This has to stop!"

She left Michael and Vincent at the house to go to Erikson's home. Vincent set Michael down on the couch. Mrs. Lenwood treated his blood-stained wounds. The slight sting of liquid on Michael's cuts was minor compared to the pain before. Mrs. Lenwood, having medical experience, also stitched up his nasty gash.

"Do you think this Alban Erikson will listen to Michael's mother?" Mr. Lenwood asked.

"I hope he does," said Vincent.

Mrs. Lenwood finished by bandaging the stitches. "Before we came, we kept worrying that Michael had changed for the worse. He didn't. He's here, with us. It surprises me that those people he knew were after him. They don't know who they're after."

"Sometimes man can behave worse than the beast he hunts," said Vincent in a grim tone.

Michael only listened to part of their conversation before falling asleep. The pain and exhaustion took their toll. But as he closed his eyes, a feeling of unexpected happiness came over him. He was back home, safe and sound, with the people who knew and protected him.

The Miracle

THE DAYS BECAME SHORTER AND COLDER, MARKING THE LATTER days of autumn. The Lenwoods wished they could stay, but their careers forbade them to do so. They promised to return as soon as possible.

Like Michael, Vincent had hope after what had happened in the quarry. Both friends were happy, but that happiness did not last long. Christmas was coming, and they had yet to find something that would break Michael's curse. With the passage of time, Vincent's faith waned with the warm weather. One day, as he was returning home from an errand, he decided to stop by Michael's house. But before he entered the yard, a bad feeling came upon him. Something did not feel right. Curious to know what it was, he went behind the house. He found Alexander standing on the snow-covered mound, staring off into the distance. The dog was shivering.

"What's wrong, Alexander?" Vincent asked him.

When Alexander heard his voice, he whined. There was something off in the distance. Squinting his eyes, Vincent saw Mr. Erikson walking alongside a ditch. He was holding a gun!

"Is he after Michael?" Vincent inquired nervously.

Alexander whined again. Vincent looked back out to the ditch. He saw Michael running towards the house. Mr. Erikson aimed his gun. Alexander knew he was going after Michael again and tried to warn Vincent. Michael was out in the open, there was no place to hide! Vincent thought Erikson said he would end the hunt, and yet there he was!

The gun fired. Even though the bullet did not hit Vincent, he felt a surge of pain in his mind when he heard the scream of a fox. He watched as his best friend tumbled into the shallow snow. Michael immediately stood back up and limped towards the house. This time it was his hind left leg that was wounded. Erikson prepared to fire another shot.

One more and the hunt would be over.

Vincent did not want that to happen. He did not care about his own safety. He ran out to where Michael was limping away from Erikson. "Don't shoot!" he cried.

Mr. Erikson growled. Vincent had never heard him growl like that before.

"Vincent! What are you doing? Get out of the way!"

"I'm not going to let you kill my friend!" said Vincent.

Erikson stomped over in fury. "What is wrong with you? I almost shot you! That fox was mine!"

"Why do you want to kill him so badly?" Vincent questioned.

Cursing under his breath, Mr. Erikson spat on the ground. "He killed one of my geese. No animal takes what is mine and gets away with it. He also bit one of my friends. That thing's cruel, now move out of the way!"

Vincent was confused. After the first incident, Michael had not been on Erikson's land. And Vincent was not aware of Michael attacking Erikson's friend. It sounded more like an act of defense rather than aggression.

"Are those the only reasons? Or is there something else? You're not hunting for food or protection. What is it?" Vincent asked.

Erikson took a step closer to Vincent. Vincent shielded Michael with his legs. All Michael could do was stay still and hope for the best.

"You ask me that?" said Erikson. "Very well, I'll tell you; no animal takes what is mine. But also, it's the pleasure of hunting. If you ever hunted yourself, you would understand."

"I have hunted before, but why do you find pleasure in taking life?" asked Vincent. "I understand if you hunt for good reason, and I understand if you try to protect what is yours. But this fox took just one goose, and that was almost five months ago. Why do you find pleasure in killing?"

"That fox is just an animal, Vincent," said Erikson. "It's no real loss if you kill one."

Infuriated, Vincent kicked the frozen ground. "Put down that gun of yours and think about what you just said!" ... "This fox is Michael!"

Erikson looked down at the fox, confused. "What do you mean?"

"This fox that you are about to kill is Michael, the very same Michael you once saved!"

"That's impossible," scoffed Erikson.

Vincent turned and looked down at Michael. A spot of blood oozed out of the fox's leg. Michael groaned with each breath. The wound looked serious.

"How can Michael be this fox?" asked Erikson.

"He was cursed. It happened while I was coming home from my uncle's. Think about it, have you seen Michael at all since I came home?"

Mr. Erikson did not answer him.

"I thought so. And when did you start seeing this fox? It was after I came home. This fox is Michael. I'm telling the truth."

Mr. Erikson kept his eyes on Michael. The fox tried to stand, but fell back on his side, wailing from the wound. Very slowly, Erikson lowered his gun. With the strength Michael had, he looked up at him. Vincent took a step back. It was now just Michael and Alban.

"No," Erikson mumbled. "No. It can't be." But it was.

Erikson dropped his gun in the snow. Crouching in front of Michael, he started to sob. He said nothing, but just shivered in the snow. He sobbed until his face was pale and white.

"I'm sorry," he finally whispered in raspy voice. "I'm so sorry."

All of his pride had crumbled. Just thinking about the times Michael had nearly died was too much for him to handle. He walked away in sorrow and regret.

When he was gone, Vincent picked up the gun and unloaded it, then he inspected Michael's wound. It looked like the bullet had grazed him. The wound had to be addressed right away. Michael's mother was not home, so Vincent helped Michael himself. He cleaned the mud and blood from his friend's coat. "First your right leg and now your left," he said lightly.

Michael sighed. He was miserable at the reminder.

"I don't think Mr. Erikson will go after you anymore. That's good. You're not in danger anymore."

Michael did not feel any better.

"I know how you feel, Michael. When I saw you get shot, I was more scared than I've ever been. I wish there was a way to lift your curse, but I don't know how." A lump formed in Vincent's throat. There was a fearful thought in the back of his mind. For the first time since he gave up the search for the witch in the park, it resurfaced. "I haven't thought about this in a while, but I think there is no way out of this. I think… you will have to be a fox for the rest of your life…"

That thought repeated itself in Vincent's mind. He did not know what to think. Leaving Michael to rest, he decided to go for a short walk.

The evening was quiet and the air was clear. A light snowfall reminded the valley that Christmas was two days away. As troubled as Vincent was, he stopped on the side of the road and knelt down, lost in his mind. If such evil could turn his friend into a fox, then there had to be a way to turn that around. All that was needed was a miracle, but that was difficult to believe. Opening his eyes again, Vincent saw the flicker of many candles from a menorah in a nearby house. The front door opened and a woman approached Vincent. The woman was Mrs. Strauss. She had lived alone as a widow for four years now. She was a kind and wise woman who loved everyone and everything.

"I saw you kneeling from outside my window," she said. "Is something troubling you, Vincent?"

Vincent fought the lump in his throat. "It's Michael. He's been having such a hard life lately. I don't know what to do to help him."

Mrs. Strauss placed a hand on Vincent's back. "I haven't seen Michael in a while. Whatever it is, it must be awful."

Vincent swallowed hard. "It is. I don't know what to do. I feel that I should accept that there is no help."

"Well then, do you have faith that Michael will find a way to overcome his troubles?" Mrs. Strauss asked.

"I once did, but there is no way."

Mrs. Strauss helped Vincent to his feet. "You know, faith without acting does not work. If you have faith that Michael will find his way, then find a way to make it happen."

"But Michael is going through things not many people know about. I can't help him."

"As a friend, you actually help a lot," said Mrs. Strauss. "But someone can help him out of his mess. Some people have special authority. If there is evil in Michael's life, it can be reversed."

Those words gave Vincent an idea. A spark was relit in his heart. The new faith kindled it until a flame of hope burned brightly. "I think I have an idea that might work. Oh, thank you, Mrs. Strauss! You're a kind person!"

Mrs. Strauss said nothing more and returned to her home. Vincent ran all the way back to Michael's house. Michael woke with a start when Vincent ran in.

"Michael! There *is* something that can be done!"

When he said this, Michael listened closely. He sat up on the couch, his tail wagging. Vincent had never seen a fox's tail wag like that before. Michael wondered what Vincent was going to do.

Vincent wrote a short note to Michael's mother, telling her that he was taking Michael out for a while (he did not say where). When he finished, he beckoned Michael to follow him. Michael limped, so Vincent carried him instead. First, Vincent returned to his house and told his parents that he had to go somewhere. His parents were confused, but they were told that it was for Michael's sake. Michael laid on the passenger seat of the car, as he had done when he first came home. Vincent did not care about the late hour. He drove back to Michael's house and grabbed a set of pajamas, then he drove all night, back to the city where it had all started. It was after midnight when Vincent reached the city. It was quieter in the night, even on the early Christmas Eve morning. Vincent drove quickly to a particular place. To many, it was just a simple home. Vincent knew the man who lived there had a special duty in life. Many scoffed at him, but Vincent knew better. The man he was seeking was a Patriarch. Taking Michael in his arms, Vincent stepped onto the porch and knocked on the door. Michael felt a little nervous being here, but not scared. He did not know exactly where he was. He did not even know that he had returned to the city where he had been cursed in the first place.

A light flickered on inside the house and an elderly woman answered the door. She looked skeptically at Vincent, carrying a wounded fox in his arms.

"Can I help you?" she asked.

Vincent mentioned the Patriarch's name. The woman raised her eyebrows in surprise. "Actually, my husband is awake. Is he expecting you?"

Vincent sadly shook his head. The woman was about to say something else when somebody came down the stairs behind her. It was the Patriarch!

"Actually, I was expecting him," said the old man.

Vincent saw a peculiar light in the Patriarch's eyes. He could be the very person that may end Michael's trial!

"Come up stairs with me, and bring the fox."

At a loss for words, Vincent followed him up the stairs. The Patriarch stopped outside the door to a small room. Vincent placed Michael on the floor and returned to the car to grab the set of pajamas. As he passed the Patriarch's wife, she smiled at him. Such a warm smile she had. When Vincent returned to the doorway of the upstairs room, he gave the clothes to the Patriarch. "How did you know I was coming?" he asked.

"Well, I will tell you," the Patriarch began. "For the last week, I dreamt that I was standing in front of a young man, then he became a fox. And then both the young man and the fox were standing next to each other. In my dream I knew they were the same person. They had the same light behind their eyes. I had this dream for six days straight, and now I know why."

Vincent was almost too afraid to ask the question on his mind. "Can… you lift his curse?"

The Patriarch stared deep into Michael's eyes. Michael stared back. There was definitely hope now.

"That's up to your friend to decide."

Michael kept his eyes on the Patriarch, not blinking once. The Patriarch then went into the small room. Michael started to follow, grunting in pain as he limped. He turned and looked up at Vincent one last time. Both his and Vincent's hearts were heavy. The Patriarch closed the door once Michael was inside. Vincent remained out in the hall. After a long wait, the Patriarch left the room. Vincent did not see Michael at all.

"It will take a few minutes," said the Patriarch after he had closed the door. "Have a seat and talk with me."

He and Vincent sat down on some chairs outside the room.

"What your friend has been through did not only affect him, did it? It looks like you have suffered as well."

"I have indeed," replied Vincent. "Having Michael, my friend… cursed to be a fox… It's very hard to think about, even now that five months have gone by. There were some people who kept trying to kill him. Twice did I see Michael nearly die. It was horrible."

The Patriarch listened closely. "Man has a special gift, but it is pride that shows the beast in us. We have instincts of our own, you know."

"So I've noticed. This has been a hard five months."

"And how was Michael cursed?" asked the Patriarch.

Vincent told him about visiting the witch. He remembered that he did not even consider drinking what the witch had given him. Michael was reluctant too, but he had taken a sip anyway.

"I see," said the Patriarch when Vincent finished his story. "It sounds like Michael was meddling with things he shouldn't have meddled with, and he learned the hard way because of it. But you must know, we all have had things that happen in our lives. We all have done wrong, or have made poor choices. I have. You have. The hunters have. Michael has. But with hope, and acting on that hope, the wrong can be overcome. The wrong becomes the right."

Vincent understood the Patriarch's words. He and the Patriarch sat in silence when the door to the room opened. Michael stood there, wearing his pajamas. His face was pale, his ears and hands were still black, and his back was hunched. There was still some fur on his arms, but most of it had shed onto the floor. His current appearance did not matter; his dreadful curse was lifted! Vincent came up and hugged him.

"I'm here," said Michael, keeping weight off his hurt leg. He turned to the Patriarch. "Thank you so much. I never thought I would live like this again. Oh, thank you!"

"Miracles do happen," said the Patriarch. "Don't worry about your hands or your ears. Your natural color will eventually return."

Michael thanked the Patriarch over and over again for lifting his curse, and he thanked Vincent for being a faithful, loyal, and reliable friend. He would have lived the rest of his life as a fox had it not been for Vincent's courage. They did not stay long though, for Michael was very tired and a little sick. He limped back to the car after one more farewell and a wish of a merry Christmas to the noble man.

"How do you feel?" asked Vincent once they were outside.

Michael groaned. "I'm getting better. Consider it good tidings, in due time anyway." He was about to open the car door when he heard somebody call his name in the distance. Mr. and Mrs. Lenwood ran up to them.

"Michael, it's you!" exclaimed Mr. Lenwood. "How did you change back?"

"Vincent helped me," said Michael. He opened the door and sat in the passenger seat, keeping the door open. He needed to stay off his wounded leg.

"What was life as a fox like?" asked Mrs. Lenwood.

Michael remembered all of his experiences of the past five months. "To tell you the truth, inside, I didn't change much. Of course, I had the instincts of a fox. The smell of a rabbit was as pleasant as an oven-cooked roast would be to a hungry human. My senses were sharp. I could see, hear, smell, and feel more keenly as a fox."

"We thought you'd become rabid," said Mr. Lenwood regretfully.

"I remember hearing you saying that in the motel room. To tell you the truth, I was scared that I'd lose myself. I stood there, staring at the corner of the room. I was too scared to do anything for those first few minutes. My instincts changed for sure, as I've said, but my mind itself didn't. Nothing was lost when I was cursed. I wasn't really gone."

"It looks like all is well," said Mrs. Lenwood, with tears in her eyes.

"It's good to see you again, Michael," added Mr. Lenwood. He shook Michael's hand while Mrs. Lenwood hugged him and kissed him on the forehead. They left him and Vincent in peace, seeing how drowsy Michael was.

"And now for home," said Vincent.

Michael was about to close the door when he noticed someone else walking across the street. The witch!

Michael and Vincent stared at the one who had caused all the trouble in the first place. When she noticed them, she had a look of shock, then anger, then defeat. She did not approach them. She walked away, a coward.

And that was the last they ever saw of the witch. Michael closed his eyes as he and Vincent left for home.

On the way, Michael thought about Mr. Erikson. It still scared Michael how the man had almost ended his mortal life on several occasions. But hatred was no remedy for it, mercy was. Michael forgave Mr. Erikson.

Vincent and Michael passed through a forest on their way home. Michael woke up when Vincent slowed down.

"Michael, look ahead."

Michael looked at where Vincent was pointing. There was a fox there, staring at them. Michael opened the door and the fox approached him. It did not say anything, but Michael knew who it was. He reached for its paw; its fur was warm and soft. The fox smiled, then vanished.

"What was that?" Vincent asked.

Michael smiled. "A friend of mine."

Vincent decided to wait and ask about it tomorrow. He let Michael sleep. Michael slept peacefully for the rest of the ride home, with the following phrase on his mind:

All is well.

The End

For more information about
Fairy Tales, Fables & Other Short Stories
and other works by Jordan B. Jolley,
be sure to visit
www.thetalesofdraco.wordpress.com

www.ingramcontent.com/pod-product-compliance
Lightning Source LLC
LaVergne TN
LVHW040319250825
819473LV00015B/116/J